THE COSMIC NETWORK OF KALKI

THE COSMIC NETWORK OF KALKI

SATISH KUMAR SAMPATHKUMAR

PAPER TOWNS
PUBLISHERS

PAPER TOWNS
PUBLISHERS

First published by

Papertowns Publishers
72, Vishwanath Dham Colony,
Niwaru Road, Jhotwara,
Jaipur, 302012

The Cosmic Network of Kalki

ISBN Print Book – 978-93-6185-657-0

Cover Design by Vidhisha Sharma
Instagram- @nivarts_
Email- vidhishasharma95@gmail.com

Printed in India

Contents

CHAPTER 1

The Silent Infiltration

The night was quiet, but Kalki knew silence could be deceptive. From a distance, the high-security facility looked like an ordinary research compound—rows of concrete buildings under the floodlights, guards pacing the perimeter with rifles slung across their shoulders. To an untrained eye, it was mundane, almost boring. But Kalki had learned that the ordinary façade was often the best disguise for extraordinary danger. Beneath that surface, he sensed something far more dangerous, something hidden in the layers of secrecy that had drawn him here tonight.

He crouched in the shadows of the tree line, his breathing steady, his gaze calculating. The crickets sang their restless chorus, and every gust of wind stirred the tall grass like ripples across a dark sea. Kalki did not move. He studied the guards' rhythm, noting every detail—the pause of a step, the shift of a rifle strap, the careless glance at a wristwatch. Each movement was a piece of a larger pattern. He had been trained to notice what others overlooked, to see in the mundane the design of control.

The compound was a labyrinth of control and deception. Its barbed fences glistened with dew, and at regular intervals, motion sensors blinked with quiet menace. The very air felt charged with the hum of invisible frequencies, a reminder of the surveillance net that hovered unseen. Somewhere within those buildings, the secret that had eluded governments, corporations, and rival agencies for decades was being harnessed. It was not simply technology. It was power—knowledge drawn from an ancient source, reframed in the cold efficiency of modern science.

Kalki adjusted the strap of his pack and closed his eyes briefly. He remembered his guru's words: *Numbers are the language of the universe. The rishis saw it first; the scientists rediscover it now.* The number **108**, sacred across centuries, echoed in his mind. One universe, zero emptiness, eight infinity—the cycle complete. The beads of a mala, the rotations of planets, even the codes hidden in DNA all reflected this pattern. He suspected that the research facility's encryption protocols, rumored to be "cosmically inspired," were not mere myth. And if the whispers were true, then tonight's mission was not just about espionage. It was about protecting the cosmic balance.

A guard stopped to light a cigarette, cupping the flame against the wind. Kalki seized the pause. In silence, he moved from the tree line into the grass, his body low, his steps soft. His training made him a ghost, his presence absorbed by the darkness. The ancient warriors of the Ramayana and Mahabharata had taught concealment as a science long before modern militaries coined terms like "stealth." He thought of Hanuman leaping unseen across the seas, of Arjuna cloaking his intent before a decisive strike. He was merely extending their legacy into a new battlefield—the shadows of espionage.

The perimeter fence loomed before him. Razor wire curled like the fangs of a sleeping serpent, daring intruders to test its bite. But Kalki had no intention of testing. From his pack, he withdrew a compact device—a fusion of modern engineering and ancient principle. The tool was calibrated to disrupt the frequency of the electric current for precisely **21 seconds**, a span chosen not by chance but by design. Twenty-one was a number of offering, a number of respect. Just as devotees offered 21 fruits, 21 lamps, 21 prayers to invoke divine blessings, so too did this device offer 21 seconds of silence to slip past the barrier.

He clipped the device to the fence and pressed the switch. The current's hum faded, the deadly wires inert. Kalki bowed his head briefly—not out of superstition, but in acknowledgment. Every act, even an intrusion, required balance. He scaled the fence swiftly, landing on the other side with a feline grace. The device blinked once, then dissolved its own circuits. By the time the current returned, there was no trace of tampering.

Inside the compound, the air felt different. Heavy, charged, as if the very atmosphere resisted intrusion. Buildings loomed like silent sentinels, their glass windows reflecting slivers of moonlight. The guards' footsteps echoed in choreographed precision. The design reminded Kalki of the *Chakravyuha*—the ancient spiral formation from the Mahabharata. Abhimanyu had once entered such a formation but could not escape. Kalki tightened his jaw. He would not repeat that fate.

He slid into the shadows of an auxiliary building, pressing his back to the cool concrete wall. His earpiece crackled faintly—his handler's voice, calm but urgent.

"Kalki, visual confirm. You're inside?"

"Yes," he whispered.

"Good. The main archive is in Sector Three. Two guards at the entrance, motion sensors inside. Cameras blind for 108 seconds every twelve minutes. You'll need to align with the next cycle."

"Understood."

Kalki checked his watch. The alignment of time mattered—108 seconds could mean the difference between revelation and capture. Numbers again. They were not coincidence. They were patterns waiting to be read.

The timing had to be perfect. The guards' patrol routes overlapped in a cycle of twelve minutes, but the surveillance cameras were designed to reset themselves for exactly one-hundred-and-eight seconds during that interval. To most infiltrators, the figure would seem arbitrary—a byproduct of coding. But to Kalki, it was confirmation. Whoever had designed this system had not only known of the number's sacred significance but had deliberately embedded it into the very fabric of the compound's security.

He crouched low, letting his gaze sweep across the courtyard. A pair of guards passed by in synchronized motion, rifles catching a glint of moonlight. Their chatter drifted into the night air, casual but edged with the tension of routine. Guards rarely relaxed on assignments like this. Kalki suspected that even they didn't know the full weight of what they were guarding, but their instincts told them enough: whatever was hidden here was worth dying—or killing—for.

When the guards turned a corner, Kalki exhaled softly and slipped across the open ground, every step calibrated to avoid loose gravel. His mind was a symphony of focus: breath, heartbeat, footsteps, shadow. Nothing wasted, nothing hurried. This was the art his ancestors had mastered. It was the same art Arjuna had honed when piercing the eye of a moving bird in Draupadi's swayamvara—unwavering concentration.

He reached the northern side of Sector Three, a squat building with reinforced walls. From this angle, the structure resembled more of a bunker than a laboratory. The faint hum of servers emanated through the ventilation shafts. Somewhere inside, secrets pulsed like a second heartbeat, hidden from the world.

He checked his watch again. The blind spot cycle would begin in less than thirty seconds. His handler's voice returned, low and deliberate.

"Stand by, Kalki. You'll have one chance at this. No second entry."

"One is all I need," Kalki murmured.

He crouched beneath a security camera. Its lens swiveled in a mechanical arc, the red light blinking with unwavering precision. The countdown began. At the exact second, the light froze, then dimmed. For one-hundred-and-eight seconds, the eye was blind.

Kalki sprang into motion. His hands found the ledge of the ventilation shaft, and in a single motion, he hoisted himself upward. The shaft's grate was secured by six bolts, but his tool made quick work of them. With a faint metallic sigh, the grate loosened, and Kalki slipped inside, vanishing from the courtyard.

The shaft was narrow and suffocating. Metal walls pressed in on either side, the air stale with the scent of dust and oil. He crawled forward, each movement calculated. In his mind, the passage became symbolic—the *cave of tapasya*, where sages withdrew into silence to find truth. For him, the silence was both an ally and a test. His heart drummed in his ears, a reminder of the finite seconds slipping away.

Halfway through, a faint red laser grid appeared ahead, crisscrossing the passage. He froze, muscles taut. Sensors, thin as spider silk, ready to trigger alarms at the slightest breach. He studied them carefully. The spacing, the angles—none of it was random. The grid was built in patterns of **21 lines**, each intersecting with another. Again, the number. Twenty-one was the cycle of offerings, of dedication, of invoking blessings.

He almost smiled. Whoever had designed this security system understood more than mathematics. They were blending ritual with technology, dharma with machinery. The universe's ancient language was hidden even here, inside steel and code.

Drawing a deep breath, Kalki shifted his weight and began to maneuver through the grid. His body moved with serpentine fluidity, every muscle under control. One slip, and the silent alarms would awaken a hornet's nest of armed soldiers. Sweat traced the side of his temple, but his focus was absolute. Inch by inch, he wove through the twenty-one beams, until the last shimmer of red was behind him.

The shaft ended at a vent above a dimly lit corridor. He peered down. Two guards stood at the far end, their posture lazy but their weapons steady. Beyond them, a reinforced door glowed faintly under the overhead light. That was the archive. The heart of the compound.

Kalki's fingers tightened on the grate. He had reached the gateway, but the challenge was only beginning.

He remembered stories his mother had told him as a child—of Abhimanyu in the *Chakravyuha*. The young warrior had entered the deadly spiral, fearless, but without the knowledge of how to escape. Kalki had no intention of repeating that fate. He would enter with clarity, and he would leave with the knowledge.

His watch ticked. The blind cycle was ending. The cameras would awaken. The window had closed.

Now he would have to improvise.

The corridor below stretched like a vein of concrete and steel, pulsing faintly with the hum of hidden servers behind its walls. At the far end, two guards leaned casually against the reinforced door, but Kalki knew better than to underestimate them. The stillness in their posture was deceptive—soldiers trained for precision often appeared relaxed until the moment action demanded otherwise.

The grate beneath Kalki's hands vibrated softly. The cameras were alive again, scanning the corridor with unfeeling patience. His chance of a clean drop was gone. He exhaled, forcing his body into stillness. A warrior who panicked was already defeated. Arjuna had once frozen on the battlefield of Kurukshetra, overwhelmed by the enormity of war, until Krishna had reminded him of his dharma. Kalki let that memory steady him now.

What is your dharma here? he asked himself. *To reveal the truth. To protect the balance. To walk into the heart of deception and emerge with light.*

His hand brushed against the inside of his pack, finding the smooth contours of a cylindrical capsule. He pressed a recessed switch, and the capsule expanded silently into a small, spider-like drone. Its eyes blinked a faint blue.

"Go," he whispered.

The drone clung to the vent wall, then slipped through the grate, crawling down with insect-like grace. From his wristband, a screen flickered to life, feeding him the drone's perspective. The guards remained oblivious as the device scuttled past their boots. It paused at the reinforced door, projecting a faint scan of its locking mechanism. Layers of code shimmered into view—overlapping encryption matrices, far beyond ordinary security.

Kalki's jaw tightened. This was not the work of ordinary engineers. The algorithm was structured in cycles of 108 iterations, each interlinked like beads of a mala. Whoever designed this had embedded cosmic order into the mathematics.

He typed a silent sequence into his wristband. Lines of code cascaded like falling water, his mind parsing symbols faster than most could comprehend. For him, this was not hacking. This was recitation, mantra made digital. Each sequence corresponded to patterns of sound and number that sages once uttered in meditation. Where others saw equations, he saw resonance.

The door's lock pulsed once. Twice. Then it stilled.

Access achieved.

But entry was not enough. The guards were still there, their rifles glinting faintly in the sterile light. Kalki studied them through the drone's lens. Their routine was predictable—one shifted his weight every 21 seconds, the other adjusted his grip in cycles of 108 breaths. Small, human patterns, unconscious but reliable.

He waited, patient as a coiled serpent. The moment came. One guard stepped away to light another cigarette, shielding the flame from the draft. The other glanced down at his wristwatch, distracted for a heartbeat.

Kalki moved.

The grate opened silently, and his body dropped like a shadow into the corridor. He landed behind the nearest guard, his arm coiling around the man's throat in a precise lock. No noise escaped—only a faint struggle, then silence. The body eased to the floor, unconscious.

The second guard turned, alarm flashing in his eyes, but Kalki was already there. A swift strike to the solar plexus stole the breath from his lungs, and a follow-up blow behind the ear ended the confrontation. Both bodies lay crumpled in silence, their rifles untouched. Kalki dragged them to the side, arranging them behind a supply crate, out of the surveillance path.

He stood before the reinforced door, its surface cool and unyielding. Behind it lay the archive—the reason for his mission. He pressed his hand to the panel. It blinked once, recognizing the bypass sequence the drone had already seeded. The lock hissed softly, and the door parted.

Inside, the air was cooler, humming with the rhythm of machines. Rows of servers blinked in synchronized patterns, their lights resembling constellations trapped in cages of steel. Screens glowed faintly, displaying streams of encrypted data. The space felt less like a laboratory and more like a temple—an altar to knowledge, concealed from the unworthy.

Kalki stepped inside, his senses sharpened. He could feel it—layers of information, hidden truths, currents of power flowing like rivers behind the screens. Somewhere within this maze of code was the secret he had come for.

And yet, as he moved deeper, he felt an unsettling presence. Not human, but something else. The air was too still, the silence too absolute. He had walked into sanctuaries before, but this was different. This was the silence of a place that guarded itself.

His wristband pulsed with a faint alert. Not from his handler. Not from the drone. Something else. A signal, faint but deliberate, echoing through the server walls.

It repeated in intervals. **108... 108... 108...**

Not random. Not accidental. A pattern. A call.

Kalki's pulse quickened. He had expected resistance, but this was something else. This was not just technology. This was invocation.

The repetition of **108** was not a mere glitch in the system—it was deliberate. Each pulse carried a frequency, faint but structured, like a mantra whispered by the servers themselves. Kalki froze, his mind racing. He had studied ancient texts, cross-referenced them with quantum mathematics, and he knew this cadence. It was the same rhythm encoded in the *Gayatri Mantra* recited 108 times, the same count used in yoga to complete cycles of breath. The system wasn't simply protecting information; it was *chanting*.

He moved deeper into the archive, rows of servers stretching endlessly like the pillars of a hidden temple. Blue and green lights blinked in perfect intervals. In that sterile glow, he felt something uncanny—an ancient resonance inside modern steel. This was no coincidence. Someone had bound sacred patterns to cold machines, invoking cosmic numbers to construct digital fortresses.

At the heart of the archive stood a single console, elevated on a dais of glass. It resembled an altar more than a workstation. On its surface, streams of symbols cascaded, not binary, but a hybrid of

Sanskrit syllables and quantum code. He leaned closer, and his breath caught—the words were fragments of the *Rig Veda*, mapped into encryption strings.

His wristband vibrated. His handler's voice cut in, tense.

"Kalki, do you have visuals?"

"Yes."

"Retrieve whatever you can. But be careful. The intel suggests the system is adaptive."

Adaptive. The word chilled him. An adaptive system that *prayed* in cycles of 108 was not simply AI. It was something else.

He touched the console. The screen flared, and the hum of servers rose, as if acknowledging his presence. A question appeared, written in ancient script:

"Dharma or Adharma?"

Kalki stiffened. The system wasn't requesting a password. It was *testing him.*

Memories surged—his guru's lessons, the stories of Mahabharata and Ramayana. Arjuna on the battlefield, torn between duty and doubt. Rama leaving Ayodhya to honor dharma above comfort. Every avatar of Vishnu had confronted this question in some form. And now, here it was—posed by a machine built on the language of rishis.

He whispered the answer, steady and firm. "*Dharma.*"

The screen pulsed. Lines of code unraveled like the petals of a lotus, opening pathways he could scarcely comprehend. Streams of information flooded into his wristband, downloaded in encrypted bursts. Files on biogenetics, quantum networks, weaponized frequencies—all interlaced with mythological algorithms.

But among them, one file glowed differently. Its name: **Project 21**.

He tapped it open. The document revealed a chilling blueprint—an experiment that merged human consciousness with quantum architecture. Subjects were placed in ritual chambers where offerings were made in cycles of **21**, echoing ancient Hindu practice. The hypothesis: that collective devotion could be harnessed, coded, and weaponized into a frequency strong enough to influence thought on a global scale.

Kalki's stomach tightened. This wasn't science—it was weaponized faith. They were trying to bend the essence of belief itself, using sacred numbers as tools of control.

The console buzzed again. A new phrase appeared:

"Will you complete the offering?"

A trap. He knew it instantly. Accepting meant activating whatever hidden protocol was tied to the ritual cycle. Refusing might trigger defenses of another kind.

His wristband blinked red—time was running out. The guards would soon rotate back, and his 108-second window to escape was narrowing.

He reached into his pack, withdrawing a small vial of sacred ash. His guru had given it to him, not as superstition but as grounding—a reminder of impermanence. He placed a single pinch on the console. Not 21 items. Not a ritual of compulsion. Just one act of balance.

The screen flickered violently. The servers wailed in unison, lights flashing like constellations exploding. Then, silence.

The console dimmed, but not before flashing a single phrase across the screen:

"You are seen."

Kalki's breath caught. The system had acknowledged him—not as an intruder, but as a participant. Whoever had built this network was aware of him now. Somewhere, beyond these walls, eyes had opened.

His handler's voice returned, sharper this time.

"Kalki, extraction now. You've triggered something."

"I know."

He downloaded the final packets of data, then turned and slipped back toward the vent. His movements were swift but controlled. Behind him, the archive seemed to breathe, as if alive. The air vibrated with a subtle chant, almost inaudible—*Om… Om…*

Om…—as though the facility itself were reciting mantras to cleanse his intrusion.

He climbed back through the vent, retraced his path past the laser grid, and descended into the night. The fence awaited, its hum alive again, but his device gave him another twenty-one seconds of passage. He crossed as silently as he had entered.

The trees embraced him once more, their shadows shielding him. He paused, turning back. The compound stood still under floodlights, guards unaware of what had transpired within. But Kalki knew. He had not simply stolen data. He had awakened something.

As he vanished into the forest, the numbers echoed in his mind—108 and 21—two keys to the cosmos, now twisted into tools of power. His mission had only just begun.

CHAPTER 2

The Trap

The cell was silent, but it was not empty.

Silence in such places was never pure; it was layered with intent, with menace. The concrete walls absorbed sound, thick with dampness and the stink of rusting metal. The single bulb overhead flickered in irregular spasms, casting shadows that crawled across the floor like restless insects. The hum of its filament was relentless, a mechanical chant that drilled into the mind, steady and cruel. Even silence, Kalki realized, could be a form of torture when laced with such repetition.

He sat against the wall, wrists bound in cold iron cuffs. The cuffs bit into his skin with every movement, their sharp edges a deliberate design to make stillness the only comfort. Each breath brought him the smell of mildew, of stagnant water that pooled in some unseen corner. His ankles were shackled too, a chain clinking faintly whenever he shifted. Somewhere beyond the cell, footsteps echoed at intervals—boots on stone, measured, unhurried. The footsteps of men who believed themselves in control.

Kalki closed his eyes. His training told him to conserve energy, but more than that, he knew the greater battle was not with chains but with the mind that surrendered to them.

Wasn't Arjuna trapped, too? The thought surfaced unbidden. Not in chains, but in the prison of despair. On the battlefield of Kurukshetra, surrounded by kin he did not wish to fight, paralyzed by doubt until Krishna reminded him of his dharma. Kalki drew strength from that memory. This was not Kurukshetra, but the principle was the same: despair was the real fetter.

He slowed his breath, inhaling deeply, exhaling longer. His ribs rose and fell with quiet discipline. The pain in his wrists dulled. The ache in his shoulders became distant. He recited inwardly verses he had memorized long ago, words etched into him beside temple fires when he was a boy:

"Your right is to action alone, never to its fruits. Be not motivated by reward, nor give in to inaction."

The lines steadied him. Chains did not define defeat. Inaction did.

The cell door groaned suddenly, iron hinges protesting. A wedge of harsh white light cut into the room, shattering the dim haze. Two guards entered, boots heavy, rifles slung carelessly yet ready. Behind them stepped a man in a black uniform, insignias on his chest that Kalki did not recognize. His movements were fluid, precise, predatory. His face was sharp, cheekbones cutting like blades, and his eyes were cold steel, glinting with satisfaction. His voice, when he spoke, was low and oily, like oil poured onto iron.

"Agent Kalki," he said, rolling the name with mock reverence, savoring it like a hunter speaking to caged prey. "A ghost in our systems. A shadow in our machines. We want to know how."

Kalki said nothing. Silence was a weapon, and he wielded it as carefully as a blade. Words could betray more than chains could hold.

The man leaned closer, his breath carrying the faint metallic tang of stimulants. "You slipped past layers that should not be breached. You saw things not meant for mortal eyes. Tell me what you saw in the archive."

For the briefest heartbeat, Kalki's pulse quickened. *He knows.* Or at least suspects. But his face remained a mask. He had learned long ago that even the flicker of an eyelid could give an enemy leverage.

"I saw nothing," Kalki replied calmly. "Just men hiding their crimes behind machines."

The man's smile was thin, a crescent of mockery. "Lies. You touched it, didn't you? The Akashic field. The web that binds thought, memory, destiny. Even your scriptures whisper of it. Don't insult me by denying."

The words sent a chill through Kalki's spine. Few outside the circles of sages and hidden orders spoke of the Akashic field. To hear it from the mouth of an enemy officer was disquieting. The prison was not mere steel and concrete; it was connected to something older, something woven into the fabric of consciousness itself.

"Our master will be eager to meet you," the man continued, straightening. "He believes you are not merely an intruder, but a key."

At his gesture, the guards moved. They slammed Kalki against the wall with brutal precision. Iron cuffs scraped his skin, tearing shallow cuts. Boots drove into his ribs, fists into his stomach, each blow calculated not to kill but to weaken. Pain flared, sharp and hot, but Kalki did not cry out. His breath hitched once, then steadied.

The officer's eyes narrowed, displeased at his resilience. He signaled the guards, and they dragged him back into the center of the cell before leaving. The door clanged shut, bolts sliding, light extinguished once more. Darkness reclaimed the room.

But the silence was no longer the same.

Symbols began to flicker behind Kalki's closed eyes. He recognized them instantly—the same ones he had glimpsed in the server room before his capture. Golden Sanskrit syllables shimmered, dancing like fire on water, interwoven with strings of binary. They floated, dissolved, reassembled, forming patterns that pulsed with hidden meaning. It was as though the network itself had followed him into captivity, projecting its visions into his mind.

He steadied his breathing. He remembered another story—Hanuman in Lanka, bound by Ravana's soldiers. His mighty tail wrapped in chains, set aflame as punishment. Yet the fire did not destroy him; it revealed his power, turning the city into ash. Chains had not weakened Hanuman. They had only proved the futility of binding one aligned with dharma.

Kalki closed his eyes fully now, retreating inward. The cuffs were cold against his wrists, but within him, heat was rising, a flame born of focus. His breath deepened, steady as a tide. The mantra rose from within, not as thought but as vibration:

Om namo bhagavate vāsudevāya.

The syllables rippled through him. They did not stay confined to his chest; they reverberated in the very walls, subtle at first, then growing. The flickering bulb above buzzed louder, its light swelling and dimming in rhythm with his chant. The concrete seemed to tremble faintly, like the skin of a drum responding to sound.

And then—vision shifted. The walls dissolved, and he was once more inside the **Cosmic Network**.

The concrete dissolved. The stench of rust and mildew vanished. The chains melted away like wax under fire. Kalki was no longer in the prison cell—at least not in the way his body perceived. He floated within a vast lattice of light and shadow, threads stretching infinitely in every direction. The **Cosmic Network** unfolded before him again, vaster now than when he had first touched it in the archive.

Each strand glowed faintly, some radiant with golden brilliance, others twisted and dark, writhing like diseased veins. Nodes pulsed like stars, each one containing fragments of thought, memory, prayer, or intention. It was beautiful and terrible, ordered and corrupted at once.

The prison was here, too—but not as concrete and steel. Before him rose a shimmering lattice, a construct of shifting patterns made from mantras and code, a doorway bound with locks that pulsed faintly in sequence. His captivity had been encoded into the very weave of the network. If he could unlock it here, he would unlock it in the material world as well.

He stepped forward—or rather, his mind projected movement, and the threads parted before him. He traced the lattice with his inner vision. Each lock was not a number or keycard, but a verse. A mantra. A sloka from the scriptures, its syllables glowing as fire-script in the void.

The first pattern gleamed with the rhythm of the **108 beads of a mala**. A circle of light, each bead a verse. To break through, he had to complete the cycle, not mechanically, but consciously, aligning thought with resonance. He inhaled and began.

"Om namo bhagavate vāsudevāya..."

The syllables left him like waves of sound, vibrating the lattice. One bead lit, then another, then another. His awareness stretched with each repetition, 108 ripples fanning outward across the web. The lattice trembled, then a lock clicked open, dispersing into starlight.

Another lock emerged, this one formed of **21 intersecting strands**, each like a path across a mandala. The offering cycle. He remembered temple rituals from childhood—the 21 lamps lit before deities, the 21 sacred leaves offered with devotion. The pattern here was no different. He extended his mind, offering not physical objects but intentions—dedications of clarity, courage, balance. Each intention lit a strand, until all 21 shone. With a resonant hum, the lock disintegrated.

The process was both effortless and exhausting. His body back in the cell strained under the pressure. Sweat beaded on his brow. His chest rose and fell sharply, though his lips moved only in whispers. Still, he pressed on.

One by one, the locks yielded. Some required him to recall verses from the *Upanishads*, others demanded concentration so precise it mirrored Arjuna aiming at the spinning fish's eye during Draupadi's swayamvara. Every lock was a trial of memory, focus, and devotion.

Finally, he reached the last barrier. It shimmered differently, half binary, half Devanāgarī script. Across it pulsed a single symbol:

धर्मम् = 101

He froze. The script was clear—*dharma.* The binary code beneath, 101, was the digital mirror of the same concept. To proceed, he had to affirm the principle not as word, but as choice.

Kalki whispered aloud, his voice steady despite the weight pressing down on him:

"*Dharma.*"

The lattice vibrated violently. The Cosmic Network pulsed as if an unseen drumbeat rolled across its threads. The cuffs on his physical wrists shattered, iron breaking with the sound of a thousand bells. Chains fell away from his ankles. His chest heaved as the resonance passed through him, collapsing the prison's bindings.

The steel door before him—both in vision and reality—groaned as though caught in an invisible current. Locks clicked in succession, five, ten, twenty-one. With a final metallic sigh, the door swung open.

The Cosmic Network shimmered, and then it receded. The cell walls returned, but the chains were gone. The stink of rust lingered, but freedom now hummed in the air like an open window.

He stepped out.

The hallway outside was empty. No guards at their posts. No footsteps. The silence was absolute, unnatural. A trap, perhaps, but he would not waste the chance.

Kalki moved forward, every sense sharpened. Each step echoed against stone, magnified by the emptiness. He recalled again Hanuman in Lanka, walking through the city even while bound, his fire destined to burn. He recalled Rama, walking alone into exile, his dharma unshaken by chains of circumstance. The stories were not fables. They were instructions.

And now, they whispered to him.

Your cycle has begun, Kalki.

Kalki stepped into the corridor, unshackled, every sense sharpened. The silence was too perfect—no cough of a guard, no scrape of boots, no murmur of radio static. The emptiness itself was a riddle.

His eyes adjusted to the dim strip-lights overhead. Their pale glow bled against walls stained with rust, each flicker in their rhythm strangely patterned. He paused. Three blinks, a pause, then another cycle. It repeated exactly **108 times** before stabilizing.

Coincidence? No. Nothing here was coincidence.

The architects of this prison had laced even its electricity with sacred cycles. To most, it would mean nothing—just faulty wiring. But to Kalki, it was a warning. Every step here was inside a system that merged the physical and the metaphysical.

He crouched low, fingers brushing the cold floor, his ears tuned. A faint hum vibrated through the concrete, as though beneath the prison walls, machines chanted their own mantra. The Cosmic Network was not confined to the archive he had breached. It was here, too, alive in the foundations of his captivity.

He remembered Abhimanyu again—the warrior prince who had entered the *Chakravyuha* formation but could not escape. This corridor was the same spiral, a trap designed not only to hold but to test. Kalki muttered under his breath:

"Not Abhimanyu this time. I will be Arjuna."

He moved with precision, each step measured. His training returned like muscle memory—the art of being unseen, the patience of waiting for shadows. A corner loomed ahead. He pressed his back to the wall and peered.

A guard slumped in a chair, rifle across his lap. His chest rose and fell in unnatural rhythm. Not sleep. Something else. Kalki's eyes narrowed. He stepped closer, every movement noiseless.

The man's eyes were open. Vacant. His lips moved, whispering a mantra without awareness:

"Om… Om… Om…"

The repetition was mechanical, not devotion. The prison itself had turned him into a conduit, a puppet chanting without faith. A bead of sweat rolled down Kalki's temple. He had heard of such states in forbidden texts—*yantra-bound minds,* where technology hijacked the nervous system and bent it into ritual.

The sight hardened his resolve. This was not merely espionage. This was desecration.

Kalki placed two fingers on the guard's pulse. It throbbed in perfect intervals—21 beats, pause, repeat. The cycle of offering twisted into control. The man was alive, but his will was shackled by numbers.

Kalki whispered a prayer for him, then moved on. To wake him might have been to trigger an alarm, or worse, to shatter a mind already enslaved. Compassion sometimes meant restraint.

The corridor narrowed, leading to a steel archway. Symbols glowed faintly along its edges—Devanāgarī script entwined with binary sequences. The words spelled fragments from the *Ramayana*:

Satyam eva jayate—Truth alone triumphs. But below, in machine code, another phrase pulsed: *Override = 108.21.*

A combination. A lock. A riddle.

Kalki closed his eyes. He remembered Rama standing at the gates of Lanka, Hanuman returning with news of Sita, the army preparing for war. The gates had not opened easily then, either. It had taken faith, strategy, and sacrifice.

He whispered the sloka again, steady:

"Satyam eva jayate."

Then, in binary, he tapped the sequence into the panel: 108.21.

The archway vibrated, humming like a conch blown before battle. With a sigh, it parted, revealing a staircase spiraling downward.

The air grew colder as he descended, shadows thickening. The hum of the Network deepened, no longer subtle but a constant undercurrent. His mind tingled with visions—threads of memory not his own, flashes of other lives, other battles. Rama stringing his bow. Krishna lifting the Sudarshana Chakra. Abhimanyu falling beneath a hail of arrows. The cycle of avatars pressed into his mind like echoes.

At the base of the stairs, another corridor stretched into darkness. He moved slowly, feeling the tension coil around him. Every instinct screamed that he was being observed—not by guards, but by the Network itself.

And then he saw it.

The walls shimmered faintly, as though covered in transparent film. Images flickered across them: his childhood by the temple fire, his guru's stern gaze, his own reflection distorted. The prison was not only made to hold the body but to probe the mind, to unravel its subject thread by thread.

For a moment, he felt the pull—an invitation to surrender, to let the walls write his destiny as code. But he clenched his fists. *No.*

He whispered Krishna's words to Arjuna:

"You have the right to action, but never to the fruits of action."

His path was clear. He was not here to be defined by the prison. He was here to define his escape.

He pressed forward, ignoring the whispers, ignoring the images. The walls dimmed, retreating into silence. Ahead, the corridor ended in another door. This one bore no lock, no code—only a symbol, vast and glowing: the Sudarshana Chakra.

A test, then. The prison would not let him leave without proving himself again.

The glowing symbol of the **Sudarshana Chakra** pulsed on the door before him, spinning slowly in golden light. Its edges shimmered with fire, sharp enough to cut thought itself. Kalki froze, awed. The Sudarshana was not merely a weapon of Vishnu; it was the wheel of time, the cycle of cosmic order, the very principle of dharma in motion. For it to appear here meant the prison had drawn its final test directly from the heart of myth.

He stepped closer. The chakra's spin grew faster, and voices whispered around him—fragments of verses, battle cries, prayers.

"Arjuna, pick up your bow..."
"Rama, cross the sea..."
"Kalki, complete the cycle..."

The voices blended into a chant, rising and falling with the rhythm of **108 beats**, echoing through the chamber like a drum of creation. The air vibrated against his skin, making his chains wounds throb with memory.

Then, another layer emerged. Twenty-one concentric circles rippled out from the chakra, each inscribed with offerings—fruits, lamps, flowers, weapons. It was both *mandala* and machine, a puzzle woven from ritual itself.

Kalki understood: to open this door, he had to align with both numbers—the infinite cycle of 108 and the complete offering of 21. If he faltered, the chakra would not simply deny him. It would devour him.

He closed his eyes. His breath steadied. He called to mind the image of Krishna on the battlefield, lifting the Sudarshana in defiance of fate. He thought of Hanuman carrying the mountain when he could not find the herb. Of Rama walking unflinching into exile. Each avatar had faced a test where surrender would have been easier than action. But dharma demanded action, not retreat.

Kalki extended his hands, palms open. He whispered the mantra that had carried him through chains and illusions alike:

Om namo bhagavate vāsudevāya.

He recited it **108 times**, each repetition lighting a spoke of the chakra. The wheel spun faster, humming with power. His body ached, but his spirit aligned with the resonance.

When the final repetition left his lips, the outer rings of the chakra blazed. Now came the offerings. He had nothing physical—no fruits, no lamps, no flowers. But devotion was not always in objects. It was in intention.

He offered twenty-one memories:

1. His first lesson by the temple fire.
2. His mother's hand on his head.
3. His guru's stern rebuke.
4. The sound of rain during meditation.
5. The warmth of sacred ash.
6. The laughter of comrades.
7. The cry of a bird in dawn silence.
8. His first wound in training.
9. His first victory.
10. His first failure.
11. A verse remembered.
12. A verse forgotten.
13. The eyes of the man he had spared.
14. The eyes of the man he had not.
15. The weight of secrecy.
16. The relief of truth.
17. The humility of bowing.
18. The pride of standing.
19. The terror of doubt.
20. The clarity of resolve.
21. The flame of dharma.

As each intention left his mind, one of the circles ignited. When the twenty-first offering blazed, the chakra let out a sound like a conch shell, triumphant and shattering. The door trembled, its frame glowing. With a roar like the sea, it split open.

Light flooded the corridor. Beyond the door lay not another cell, but the night sky itself. The prison had been a labyrinth folded within itself, a maze of mind and machine. And now, Kalki had walked its spiral, pierced its illusions, and emerged into freedom.

The forest stretched before him, the same shadows that had concealed his infiltration. The air was cool, scented with pine and soil. For a moment, he simply breathed, feeling the chains' absence on his skin.

But he knew this was not escape. This was release into the next stage. The enemy officer's words echoed in his ears: *Our master will be eager to meet you.*

He clenched his fists. Whoever this master was, they had harnessed numbers sacred to the cosmos, twisted mantras into machines, enslaved minds into chants. This was no ordinary war of nations. This was Kurukshetra reborn, the battlefield stretched across code and consciousness.

The cycle of avatars was not story—it was blueprint. Rama had fought to restore balance. Krishna had guided dharma through diplomacy and war. And now, Kalki stood where they had once stood—at the edge of a conflict that would shape ages.

He walked into the trees, shadows swallowing him. The night seemed to lean closer, listening. His path was uncertain, but his purpose was not.

The war had begun.

CHAPTER 3

Escape Through the Network

The corridor stretched ahead, silent and sterile, its white walls gleaming faintly under strips of cold light. Yet beneath the silence, Kalki could feel the faint hum of energy coursing through hidden conduits. It wasn't just electricity; it was rhythm. The walls breathed in pulses like a heartbeat.

Barefoot, he moved forward with deliberate care. Each step was soft, precise, as though he were crossing sacred ground. The broken cuffs he had left behind in the cell still pressed faintly into his skin, phantom weight lingering even in freedom. They were relics of captivity, but also of initiation. He was no longer who he had been before entering the compound.

Still, freedom here was a mirage. This place was not a prison in the old sense of chains and walls. It was a labyrinth stitched from code and concrete, surveillance and deception. He knew the architecture—mirrored glass concealing cameras, vents that whispered with hidden microphones, corners wired with motion sensors. To walk unmasked was to walk inside the enemy's gaze.

He could not simply escape. He had to vanish.

Kalki pressed his palm against the wall. The steel was cold, but beneath its surface he felt vibration. He closed his eyes and inhaled slowly, syncing his breath with the pulse. Inhale—two beats. Exhale—three beats. The hum steadied. For a moment, it wasn't hum at all.

It was chant.

Da-da-da… Om… da-da-da…

The sound fractured. His vision blurred. The white wall dissolved, bleeding into rivers of light. Sanskrit slokas appeared, glowing like molten gold, their letters shimmering against lattices of binary code. Fragments from the *Rig Veda* twisted into streams of ones and zeroes. Both systems, ancient and digital, intertwined like two serpents around a single staff.

Kalki's breath deepened. His mind stretched, not outward but inward. He recalled Krishna's words to Arjuna, words spoken at the heart of Kurukshetra:

"He who sees inaction in action, and action in inaction, is wise among men."

The verse slid into place like a key. He was not walking in a corridor. He was walking inside a body—a system alive, self-aware. And every living system had a pulse. Every pulse a weakness.

He extended his awareness into the lattice. The patterns bent to him, mantras aligning with thought, numbers reshaping into resonance. With each subtle shift, a red surveillance light winked out. One by one, the cameras died—like stars dimming at dawn.

When he opened his eyes again, the corridor was silent, truly silent. For the first time since his capture, no unseen eye watched him.

But silence is a fragile gift.

Boots thundered behind him. Three men. Trained. Rifles raised.

"Freeze!"

Kalki tilted his head, the ghost of a smile curving his lips. Their shapes reflected faintly in the polished steel door ahead, the red glow of rifle sights hovering over his back.

So this is the test, he thought. *Not stillness, but action.*

He dropped low, his movement a blur. His leg swept outward, catching the edge of a steel tray abandoned on the floor. The tray skidded across the tiles with a shriek of protest. It struck the lead guard's ankle with a crack, toppling him mid-stride.

Kalki lunged forward, snatching the man's rifle before it hit the floor. He spun it upward in a fluid arc—no wasted movement, no hesitation. Two shots barked into the corridor. Controlled. Precise. The second and third guards collapsed before their own fingers reached their triggers. Weapons clattered from their hands, echoing like dropped bells.

The fallen man scrambled to his knees, blood trickling from his temple. His hand fumbled for a sidearm at his belt. Kalki's elbow drove into his face with the precision of a hammer on an anvil. Bone crunched. Blood sprayed across the sterile white wall, a brutal signature on the canvas of silence.

The man sagged, unconscious.

Kalki exhaled. His heart pounded, but his breath remained steady. He had been taught long ago: battle was not chaos, but rhythm. To lose rhythm was to lose dharma.

The corridor shimmered faintly. For a heartbeat, it was not steel and light but a battlefield of dust and warriors. Conches blared. Horses screamed. Shadows of warriors clashed—Arjuna's chariot poised against Bhīṣma's phalanx. Kurukshetra rose in his vision, painted over the sterile prison like a veil of truth over illusion.

Then it was gone.

But his hands still trembled—not with fear, but with recognition. Each skirmish was not merely survival. It was enactment of a war older than nations.

Kalki crouched low, pressing his fingertips to the rifle he had taken. The metal was still warm from the guard's hands, its weight familiar yet foreign. He had trained with dozens of such weapons, mastered their mechanics, but tonight it was not simply a gun. It was an extension of the battlefield, an arrow in the modern Kurukshetra.

He checked the corridor again. Silent. Empty. But the silence was brittle, a thin veil stretched over the tension of alarms waiting to howl. He could not linger.

He moved swiftly, flowing down the hallway with the grace of a hunter. The architecture was designed to disorient—sterile walls repeating endlessly, corners leading into identical passages, stairwells that doubled back into themselves. It was the *Chakravyuha* again: the spiral formation into which Abhimanyu had once entered but never escaped. The enemy had designed their fortress as a mental snare as much as a physical one.

Kalki muttered under his breath:
"Not Abhimanyu. Arjuna."

The words grounded him. Abhimanyu had lacked the knowledge of the exit. But Arjuna, guided by Krishna, had pierced and escaped. That would be his path.

He reached a stairwell, its railings cold and slick with condensation. He descended in silence, every sense taut. The faint hum of circuits reverberated through the walls. It was not just electricity—it was chanting again, hidden inside frequencies. He caught fragments in the rhythm of the stairwell lights:

Da-da-da… Om… da-da-da… Om…

The pattern repeated. **108 pulses** before each reset. Even the architecture prayed in silence.

Kalki placed his hand briefly against the wall. His breath synced with the hum. He whispered:

"Om namo bhagavate vāsudevāya."

The circuits flickered, the lights dimmed for a fraction of a second—as though the building itself acknowledged him. He smiled faintly. The fortress was alive, but even living systems could be persuaded.

At the next landing, a shadow shifted. Two guards emerged, rifles raised. Their boots struck the stairs in unison, disciplined.

Kalki dove sideways, rolling behind a column. Bullets screamed past, sparking against steel. The air smelled of ozone and burnt dust.

He inhaled, slowed his heart. He thought of Rama in the forest, his bow steady as he faced demons in exile. Rama had fought not with rage, but with clarity. So too must he.

He leaned out, squeezed the trigger once. A shot cracked, clean and decisive. The first guard staggered, weapon clattering against the rail. The second fired wildly, bullets shredding plaster from the wall near Kalki's head.

Kalki slid across the floor, closing the distance like a serpent. His shoulder drove into the man's knees, toppling him. In one motion, he disarmed him and pressed the butt of the rifle against his throat. The man's breath caught. Eyes bulged. Then silence.

Both bodies slumped, unmoving. Kalki stripped their belts for ammunition, reloaded, and moved on.

But the fight was not what shook him. It was what followed.

As he stepped back into the corridor, the walls shimmered again. For a heartbeat, he was no longer in sterile concrete but standing in Kurukshetra's dust. Across from him loomed Bhīṣma, white-bearded and resolute, arrows bristling from his armor like a forest. Behind, rows of warriors surged, shouting oaths of loyalty and doom. The vision was vivid, alive, pressing into his mind like memory rather than illusion.

He blinked, and it vanished. Yet the echo remained in his bones. The prison was not merely a place. It was a battlefield stitched into time itself, replaying the great wars of dharma and adharma through its walls.

Kalki pressed on. Down another hall, through another checkpoint. Each lock he encountered dissolved at his touch, as though the codes themselves recognized him. His fingers danced over panels, whispering mantras under his breath. Where others would see numbers, he saw verses. Where others fought encryption, he aligned resonance.

At the last checkpoint, he came to a reinforced blast door. Triple authentication: fingerprint, retina, numeric sequence. Impossible for ordinary intruders.

Kalki laid his hand on the scanner. His vision blurred again. The lattice unfolded—digital knots woven with Sanskrit glyphs, guarded by serpents of black static. They hissed, snapping with jaws of corrupted code.

He thought of Hanuman before Lanka's gates. Demons had stood there, mighty rakshasas blocking the way. Hanuman had not cowered. He had spoken truth, and truth had broken their will.

Kalki whispered a single word.

"*Dharma.*"

The serpents froze, then dissolved into smoke. The locks clicked in sequence—fingerprint bypassed, retina cleared, code unlocked.

The blast door groaned, its gears grinding like ancient wheels. Slowly, it slid open. Beyond lay night.

Cool air swept across his face, carrying the scent of pine and soil. Stars glittered above, patient witnesses to his escape. For a moment, he simply stood there, drinking in the sky, the freedom.

But even freedom trembled. Deep within the compound, alarms howled. Red lights ignited. Searchlights cut across the darkness like blades. The fortress had awakened.

Kalki exhaled. His lips moved around another verse:

"Yato dharmas tato jayah."
Where there is dharma, there is victory.

And then he ran.

The night air was sharp in his lungs as Kalki burst into the open. The stars above glittered coldly, scattered across the sky like the silent eyes of ancient rishis watching the drama unfold. For a fleeting moment he tasted freedom, the unbound vastness beyond walls. But the alarms reminded him: this was not liberation. This was pursuit.

Red strobes pulsed across the compound, each burst of light painting the world in flashes of urgency. Floodlights snapped to life, their beams cutting through the dark like divine weapons cast from the heavens. Sirens wailed, metallic and harsh, the sound of a fortress awakening to war.

Kalki sprinted low across gravel, every movement a calculation. He had trained for this—breath measured, muscles uncoiling like springs, mind detached from panic. Each heartbeat was a drumbeat of dharma. Each stride, a choice against adharma.

A voice crackled through the compound's speakers, cold and commanding:

"Target on the move. All units converge."

Boots thundered. Men shouted. The growl of engines rose as armored vehicles roared to life. And above it all came the thrum of rotor blades—*whup-whup-whup*—a helicopter rising like a mechanical Garuda, sweeping its gaze across the earth below.

The first searchlight sliced across the ground, searing white. Kalki dropped into a drainage trench, body pressed into cold mud. Bullets rattled against the concrete lip, sparks spitting inches from his head. Gravel exploded under fire.

He whispered into the earth, voice steady even as lead tore the night:

"Yato dharmas tato jayah."
Where there is dharma, there is victory.

The mantra steadied him, reminding him he was not prey but participant in an eternal war.

The searchlight swept on. Kalki rose, mud dripping from his arms, and sprinted again. Ahead, wire fences glistened, coils of razor spiraling like serpents ready to strike. Beyond them loomed the forest—dark, infinite, whispering freedom.

But the fences were alive with electricity. He could see the faint shimmer of currents rippling along their length. Touch them, and death would be instant.

Kalki skidded into shadow, crouching behind a generator shack. He pressed his palm against the earth again, listening. Beneath his fingers, he felt the hum of power cycling through the fence. The rhythm was familiar—twenty-one pulses, pause, repeat. The cycle of offering, once sacred, now weaponized.

He closed his eyes, syncing breath with the pattern. Twenty-one heartbeats. He could slip through only in the pause. The window would be seconds, but it would be enough.

The ground trembled—soldiers were closing in. He had no more time.

He sprinted toward the fence, every nerve taut. Bullets cracked behind him, but he did not flinch. He counted the rhythm. Nineteen. Twenty. Twenty-one.

The hum ceased for the briefest pause. Kalki leapt. His fingers found the chain links, his body pulled upward in a surge of strength. The wire was cold but inert. He scaled it like a panther, his movements fluid.

Halfway up, the current surged again. Sparks spat from the metal, biting at his heels. He vaulted over, twisting in the air. He landed hard on the other side, knees absorbing the shock.

The earth beneath his palms vibrated with renewed electricity—the window had closed. Had he been a second slower, he would have been ash.

Shouts erupted behind him. Searchlights swung wildly, converging on his position. The helicopter banked, its beam sweeping. Kalki dove into the trees just as the light blazed across the fence. Bullets tore into bark, splinters raining across his face.

The forest welcomed him. Branches clawed at his arms, roots tangled his feet, but he pressed deeper, each stride fueled by necessity. His breath rasped, heart hammering, yet his mind remained clear. He thought of Arjuna again—alone in the battlefield, arrows darkening the sky, yet steady because dharma had to be upheld.

Leaves whispered above him, stirred by the helicopter's downwash. The machine hovered, its searchlight scouring the canopy. Kalki pressed his back against the trunk of an ancient tree, body melting into shadow. He slowed his breath, reducing himself to stillness.

The light passed.

He tilted his head back, staring at the stars through the canopy. In the gaps of leaves, he saw constellations his guru had once taught him—patterns of sages, hunters, warriors. They did not speak, but their presence steadied him. The cosmos itself was witness.

Kalki exhaled. His hands trembled not from fear but from recognition. This was not simply escape. This was initiation into a war that had been waiting for him.

And somewhere in the labyrinth of code and concrete he had left behind, something vast and ancient had recognized him as well.

The forest swallowed him whole. Shadows clung to him, branches clawed his arms, roots threatened to catch his stride, but Kalki moved as if the darkness itself guided him. Behind him, the compound roared like a wounded beast. Sirens keened, engines bellowed, orders cracked through radios. The hunt had begun.

Through the canopy came the roar of rotor blades. The helicopter swept low, its beam tearing through the forest in violent arcs. The white light slashed across trunks, illuminating the chaos of men crashing through undergrowth, rifles raised.

Kalki's muscles screamed, but he pushed harder, weaving between trees, vaulting over roots, sliding under branches. He knew that speed alone would not save him. To outrun the machine eye of the Network was impossible. He had to move differently—like a shadow, like thought itself.

Ahead, the forest opened into a clearing, moonlight spilling like silver milk across the ground. Bad terrain. He would be exposed. But retreat was death.

The helicopter's beam found him, dazzling his vision. Gunfire erupted, bullets carving furrows into the earth at his heels. Kalki dove forward, rolling across the clearing, mud and leaves clinging to his body. He came up crouched, rifle steady, eyes narrowed.

Three soldiers burst into the clearing. Their formation was disciplined, rifles raised in perfect arcs. They moved like a single organism, each step synchronized.

Kalki inhaled. His guru's words returned: *Numbers are not just measures. They are weapons.*

He counted their rhythm. Twenty-one steps between each pause. Predictable. Exploitable.

He waited until the pause came, then struck. His rifle barked once, twice, thrice. Each shot found its mark, soldiers falling like severed branches. Their formation collapsed, broken.

The helicopter swung back, spotlight pinning him. Its gun roared, spraying the clearing with lead. Bark exploded, dirt geysered, the air filled with splinters. Kalki sprinted toward a massive banyan at the clearing's edge, its roots twisting like serpents into the soil. He dove into their embrace as bullets tore into the ground where he had stood.

Pressed against the trunk, heart pounding, he whispered another mantra:

"Om namo bhagavate vāsudevāya."

The rhythm of the chant steadied his hands, slowed his breath. The banyan seemed to respond, its vast trunk humming faintly beneath his palms. In his vision, for a moment, he saw its roots stretching not just into earth but into light, connecting to the **Cosmic Network** itself.

The helicopter circled overhead, frustrated, its searchlight stabbing through branches. Kalki pressed deeper into the banyan's shadow, becoming stillness itself. Slowly, the beam moved on, sweeping across the forest, hunting but not finding.

He exhaled.

The forest beyond beckoned. He moved again, slipping between trees, his body a ghost among shadows. He ran until the alarms dimmed behind him, until the roar of the helicopter grew faint, until the only sounds were crickets and wind sighing through leaves.

At last, he stopped. He stood in a grove lit only by starlight, chest heaving, skin streaked with blood and mud. Freedom had been won—but not peace.

For even here, in the stillness, he felt it: a gaze upon him. Not human. Not machine. Something vaster.

The memory of the archive returned—the console whispering, *"You are seen."*

He understood now. The Network had marked him. It had recognized his voice, his mantras, his alignment with dharma. Somewhere, its Master knew his name, his rhythm, his pulse.

He looked up at the sky. The stars burned with quiet intensity, as if waiting. In them, he saw patterns: the bow of Arjuna, the mace of Bhīma, the wheel of Krishna. The cycles of avatars unfolding across constellations.

Kalki clenched his fists. The battle was no longer about infiltration or escape. It was Kurukshetra reborn, a war across both matter and mind. He was not just a spy. He was a participant in a cycle stretching back through ages.

The forest whispered around him, ancient and alive. Somewhere in its depths, allies or answers might wait. But the enemy was already moving, their nets tightening across earth and code alike.

Kalki stepped into the darkness, shoulders squared, breath steady. His body ached, his blood stained, but his spirit burned steady with one truth.

The war had only just begun.

CHAPTER 4

Ritual of Fire

The forest pressed close around him, dense and wet, its canopy so thick that even the moonlight seemed swallowed whole. Every breath brought with it the sharp tang of damp earth, the musk of rotting leaves, and the faint sweetness of night-blooming jasmine. Kalki moved through it like a hunted animal, body low, senses sharpened to the smallest sound. His skin was streaked with mud and blood, his ribs aching from blows that still throbbed with memory.

Behind him, faint but persistent, the alarms from the compound drifted through the night like echoes of a distant battlefield. They seemed less like machines and more like the cries of wounded soldiers—reminders that war had begun, even if the battlefield was yet to be fully revealed.

Branches clawed at his arms, thorns bit his legs, roots tried to trip his stride, but still he pressed forward. Each step was both burden and blessing: the burden of exhaustion, the blessing of survival. He moved by instinct, guided not by map or memory but by something deeper, a pull that seemed to whisper through the forest itself.

Hours passed. The darkness grew heavier, until the forest felt endless, timeless. Then, abruptly, the trees thinned. Kalki stumbled into a clearing, breath ragged, heart hammering.

At its center stood the ruins of an ancient shrine.

The sight struck him like a blow. Stone pillars leaned like weary sentinels, their surfaces cracked and half-swallowed by roots. Moss carpeted their carvings, but through the green veil he saw the figures—Rāma with his bow drawn, Hanuman leaping through the air, Krishna smiling gently as he played his flute. Time had tried to bury them, but their essence remained, stubborn and luminous.

Kalki dropped to his knees. This was not coincidence. He had been led here.

The night was silent but alive. Cicadas droned in waves, owls called distantly, and the forest exhaled around him. His body screamed for rest—muscles trembling, eyelids heavy—but his spirit demanded something else. A ritual.

He began to gather. Dry twigs, brittle branches, leaves that curled with age. He arranged them with precision, forming a square at the shrine's heart. From his pack he drew flint and steel, the ancient tools of fire-making, as though instinct itself rejected modern convenience.

Sparks kissed the tinder. Smoke curled, tentative and fragile. Then flame. A small tongue of fire licked upward, trembling in the night air.

Kalki sat cross-legged before it. The heat touched his face, the light painted his features in shifting orange. He closed his eyes, and from the depths of memory—not thought, but memory—words rose:

"Agnaye svāhā..."

The mantra flowed from his lips like water from a hidden spring. He gathered leaves and offered them into the fire. The flames accepted, crackling higher, answering his devotion.

He repeated the chant again and again, each cycle deepening his focus. He whispered it **108 times**, the sacred number of completeness, his breath syncing with the crackle of the fire. With each repetition, the flames grew, rising as though fueled not only by leaves but by intention itself.

Then he shifted. He gathered small stones, fruits from the forest floor, even droplets of water cupped from a nearby hollow in the roots. One by one, he offered them in cycles of **21**. Not because they were needed, but because the number carried weight. Devotees had always brought 21 lamps, 21 flowers, 21 fruits in rituals of dedication. Here, in this clearing, under a canopy that seemed to listen, Kalki completed the ancient cycle.

As smoke curled upward, the world began to change.

The forest wavered. The ruins blurred. The night dissolved.

He was no longer kneeling in a clearing.

He was seated at the edge of a battlefield.

Kurukshetra.

Dust roared across the plains, whipped into storms by the clash of thousands of feet and hooves. War cries thundered. The clang of steel split the air. Chariots surged like waves, arrows darkened the sky, and the earth itself trembled under the weight of destiny.

In the distance, Kalki saw Arjuna. The warrior's bow slipped from his hand, despair etched deep into his face. His shoulders sagged, his gaze dropped. He could not fight. Not against kin, not against teachers. Beside him, Krishna raised his hand—not in command, but in counsel. Calm. Patient. Eternal.

The scene shifted.

Now he saw Rāma. The prince walked barefoot through the forest, Sītā beside him, Lakshmana at his flank. Exile. Injustice. Yet their faces bore no bitterness, only resolve. Even stripped of kingdom, they carried dignity as if it were armor.

Again the vision shifted. The battles and exiles bled together, threads woven into one tapestry. Mahābhārata into Rāmāyaṇa, Rāmāyaṇa into Mahābhārata. And in their weaving, Kalki saw himself.

Spy. Warrior. Exile. Disciple.

The fire blazed higher, its flames no longer bound by wood. They roared like a living thing, as if the cosmos itself answered his realization.

Then, as suddenly as it began, the vision collapsed.

Kalki gasped and opened his eyes. He was back in the clearing, the shrine looming silently, the fire crackling at its center. The forest buzzed with life again.

But he was no longer alone.

Kalki's breath steadied as the vision faded, but the fire still blazed higher than it should have, fed by something more than dry wood.

Sparks spiraled into the night, carried upward as if messages delivered to unseen eyes. He stared into the flames, heart still pounding with the echo of Kurukshetra's war cries and Rama's footsteps through exile.

Then, the silence shifted.

A twig cracked at the edge of the clearing. A whisper of movement, too deliberate to be the forest's natural chorus. Kalki's hand went instinctively to the knife at his belt. His body coiled, ready to strike, every muscle on edge.

Out of the shadows, a figure emerged.

It was a woman, slender, wrapped in a plain shawl that clung to her shoulders damp with dew. Her hair fell loose, and her eyes glowed with an unnatural clarity in the firelight. She did not flinch under his gaze. She stood as though she had expected to find him here, as though the forest itself had guided her steps to the ruined shrine.

Kalki's grip tightened on the knife. His voice was low, steady. "Who are you?"

The woman lifted her hands slightly, palms open, her gesture one of peace. Her voice was calm, though her words carried urgency. "Not your enemy. My name is Ananya. I've been tracing the same symbols you have."

Kalki narrowed his eyes. "Symbols?"

She stepped closer, the fire painting her face in shades of orange and shadow. Her gaze flickered not to him, but to the flames. "The network isn't just wires and machines. It speaks. In Sanskrit. In code. In both at once. You've seen it, haven't you?"

The directness of her words caught him off guard. Few would dare suggest such a thing. Fewer still could. He said nothing, but his silence was answer enough.

Ananya's lips curved faintly, though it was not quite a smile. "I knew it. I thought I was losing my mind. Weeks ago, I hacked into a stream that wasn't supposed to exist—raw data, they said. But instead of strings of code, I saw verses. Hymns. Rig Veda stanzas, woven into binary like threads in a loom. I thought perhaps fatigue had twisted my perception. Until tonight." She nodded toward him. "Until I found you."

The flames cracked sharply, sparks leaping skyward as though punctuating her words.

Kalki studied her in silence. Her clothes were simple, her shawl torn in places from travel. She was not a spy; her posture lacked the hardness of training, her hands bore calluses from typing, not from combat. Yet her eyes burned with something familiar. The same fire he had glimpsed in himself when the Network had revealed its lattice.

At last, he spoke. His tone was cautious. "If you've seen what I've seen, then you also know it's not just code. Someone is shaping it."

Ananya's expression darkened. She nodded slowly. "Maya."

The name lingered in the night like smoke.

Her gaze turned distant, her voice low. "I don't know who he really is, but I know what he controls. Entire sections of the Network bend to his will. He bends reality itself, like Ravana bent illusions to confuse Rama's army. Nations follow his manipulations without realizing. Decisions of leaders, movements of armies, markets rising and falling—it's all being nudged. He's building something vast, and it's wrong."

Kalki stared into the fire. For a heartbeat, the flames shifted. In them, he thought he saw a face—dark, smiling, eyes glittering with cruelty. A phantom of their unseen enemy. A whisper of Ravana, a shadow of Duryodhana, a mask that might belong to either or to someone worse.

The fire hissed, spitting sparks, as if warning him.

Ananya stepped closer, the firelight painting her features in flickering relief. She lowered herself to the ground opposite him, folding her legs beneath her. Her eyes never left his. "You escaped tonight, but you know as well as I do—that was only the beginning. The Network doesn't let go. Not of someone like you. If you're truly who I think you are, then you can't keep running. You'll have to fight him."

Her words carried conviction, but also the weight of fear.

Kalki studied her a long while. He saw no deceit, but he saw scars—not on her skin, but in the weariness around her eyes, in the way she sat as though she had walked far carrying burdens too heavy for her frame.

He turned back to the fire. Its heat washed across his face, its pulse matched the beating in his chest. The ritual was complete, yet its meaning had only begun.

He lowered his head. His voice was quiet, but it carried into the night. "Then let the fire bear witness. I will fight. For dharma."

The flames leapt higher, illuminating the shrine's carvings—Rama with his bow, Krishna with his flute, Hanuman frozen mid-leap. Their shadows stretched long across the clearing, towering over him.

The old stories were no longer myths carved in stone.

They were instructions.

And Kalki was ready to follow them.

The fire crackled and roared, casting long, restless shadows across the clearing. For a time, neither Kalki nor Ananya spoke. The silence was not empty; it was thick, laden with the awareness of two strangers bound by the same unseen thread.

Ananya shifted slightly, her shawl slipping from her shoulder. The flames reflected in her eyes, making them seem like mirrors of the fire itself. When she finally spoke, her voice was softer, but edged with something deeper than fear—conviction.

"I didn't stumble into this," she said. "I was searching. My father… he was an archivist. He spent his life studying ancient manuscripts—Vedas, Upanishads, even obscure tantric texts. He said there were codes in them, patterns that mapped onto the cosmos itself. People laughed at him. Called him delusional. But after he died, I found his notes. And when I started working with network data streams…" She shook her head. "The same patterns were there. The same numbers. 108. 21. Repeating like a heartbeat inside the machine."

Kalki listened in silence, the words resonating with his own discoveries. She continued, her eyes fixed on the fire:

"At first, I thought it was just coincidence. But then I saw… other things. Glitches, maybe. Except they weren't glitches. I'd be working at night, and Sanskrit letters would start appearing in the code. Shifting. Rearranging. Forming verses. Sometimes, even mantras. Once, I saw the *Gayatri Mantra* written across a firewall log. Binary translating itself into prayer. That's when I knew I wasn't imagining it."

She paused, the fire's light trembling across her face. "And then… I saw him. Not clearly. Just a face in the data, as if the code itself carried his shadow. He smiled at me. As if he knew I was watching."

"Maya," Kalki said quietly.

Ananya nodded. "Maya." She drew the name out like venom. "He isn't just controlling the Network. He's infusing it with illusion. I think he's using the sacred numbers not to preserve dharma, but to twist it—to create something that looks divine, but isn't."

Kalki thought of the archive, the console's question—*Dharma or Adharma?*—and the fire's phantom face that had leered back at him. He felt the memory stir in his chest like a cold wind.

"You said he bends reality," he murmured. "Like Ravana did with his illusions."

"Yes," she said. "Only Ravana worked with palaces and shadows. Maya works with minds. He can plant thoughts, bend perceptions. Imagine an entire nation thinking a war is just, when it isn't. Imagine leaders making decisions that feel righteous, but serve only him."

The fire cracked sharply, sending sparks swirling into the sky. Both of them turned instinctively, as if expecting a response.

And in that moment, the flames changed.

They flared taller, brighter, until the clearing was awash with gold. The carvings on the ruined shrine seemed to stir, their stone eyes reflecting light. The flames twisted into shapes—not random, but deliberate.

First, a chariot, wheels blazing. Horses reared, their manes of fire scattering sparks. A figure stood atop it, bow drawn, arrow poised against an unseen foe. Arjuna. Kurukshetra's warrior.

Then the fire shifted. A palace rose, towering and proud, but its towers bent inward, impossible angles folding in on themselves. At its gates stood a figure with many faces, each smiling, each cruel. Ravana. The lord of illusions.

Ananya inhaled sharply, clutching her shawl. "It's showing us…"

"The pattern," Kalki finished. His voice was calm, but his pulse raced. He knew the fire was no ordinary blaze. It had become a mirror, a messenger. The ritual had opened a door, and through it came fragments of what lay ahead.

The flames whirled again, collapsing into a single shape. A wheel of fire, spinning endlessly, sparks flying outward in all directions. The **Chakra**—Vishnu's weapon, the wheel of time, the cycle of dharma itself. It spun faster, then slowed, until its edges began to blur. From its rim, shadows seeped outward, coiling like serpents.

Maya.

The word reverberated in Kalki's chest though it was not spoken aloud.

The wheel dimmed, and the fire settled again into its ordinary dance, crackling as if nothing had happened.

Neither of them moved. The forest seemed to hold its breath.

Finally, Ananya whispered, "He's coming for you. He already knows."

Kalki stared into the flames, his jaw tightening. "Then let him. Dharma does not flee from adharma."

She studied him, her eyes measuring, searching. "You speak like a warrior. But you're not just a warrior, are you?"

He didn't answer immediately. His gaze shifted to the carvings behind her—Rama, Krishna, Hanuman. Their stone faces seemed to glow faintly in the firelight, as if they, too, waited for his reply.

"No," he said at last. His voice was steady, but softer than before. "I am a fragment of something older. The stories they left were not tales to comfort children. They were blueprints. Instructions. And now, they are being tested again."

Ananya nodded slowly, her expression a mix of fear and recognition.

For a long moment, they sat in silence, only the fire speaking between them.

The fire had quieted, its great visions collapsing back into a steady flame, but the weight of what it had shown lingered in the air like incense after a ritual. Kalki and Ananya sat across from one another, two figures bound not by trust yet, but by destiny.

Ananya broke the silence first. "Do you know why I came here?"

Kalki's eyes narrowed. "The forest isn't kind to wanderers. You don't look like someone who stumbled into this shrine."

She shook her head. "No. I didn't stumble. I followed signals—fragments of code I couldn't trace to any server on earth. They weren't random; they pulsed in cycles. 108 pings. Then 21. Over and over again. They led me here." She gestured at the shrine. "And when I arrived, I saw your fire. As if it was waiting for both of us."

Kalki felt the words settle inside him like stones dropped into a deep pool. The numbers again. Always the numbers. Not coincidence—guidance.

"You said you've seen Maya," Kalki said. "Then you must know what he wants."

Ananya's gaze dropped, her fingers tightening around the shawl. "Control. Not just of the Network. Of thought itself. He's building something that makes illusion indistinguishable from reality. If he succeeds, dharma won't just be bent—it will be erased."

Kalki stared into the fire, its warmth pressing against his skin. He thought of Ravana's golden city, built from stolen power. He thought of Duryodhana's court, where truth was mocked and deceit enthroned. Adharma always sought to rule not through strength, but through corruption of perception.

The fire hissed suddenly, spitting sparks. In its flames, for the briefest moment, he saw again that face—smiling, eyes glinting, a presence watching him. His grip tightened on the knife at his belt.

Ananya's voice drew him back. "You don't have to fight alone."

Her tone was simple, without flourish. It was not a plea but an offering. Her shoulders were tired, her clothes ragged, but her eyes carried the same fire that burned in him.

Kalki studied her, measuring the truth in her words. He had been taught to trust sparingly, to see betrayal even in kindness. But the firelight painted her not as spy or intruder, but as ally. Someone who had glimpsed the same truth, suffered the same disorientation, and chosen to step deeper rather than retreat.

"You believe I'm who the stories spoke of," he said quietly.

Ananya hesitated, then nodded. "Not a myth. Not a prophecy. A pattern. The cycle continues, and this time, it's you."

Kalki turned to the fire. Its glow illuminated the carvings behind him—Rama with his bow, Krishna with his flute, Hanuman in mid-flight. Their shadows loomed across the clearing, long and solemn. He felt their gaze upon him, not as stone, but as presence.

He reached forward and fed another handful of leaves into the flame. The fire flared, crackling in response. His voice was low, but it carried, steady as mantra:

"Let the fire bear witness. I will not flee. I will not hide. I will fight—not for victory, not for glory, but for dharma."

The flames leapt higher, as if answering his vow. Sparks rose into the night, vanishing into the canopy like stars being born.

Ananya bowed her head slightly, her expression unreadable. "Then it begins."

The forest seemed to shift around them, the night deepening, the wind carrying a faint whisper like a warning. Kalki felt it too—the sense of a gaze fixed upon them, vast and hungry. Somewhere far beyond the clearing, in the heart of circuits and shadows, Maya stirred.

He had escaped walls of concrete and steel, but he had not escaped the Network. He had not escaped Maya.

The war was already reaching for him.

Kalki straightened, his shoulders squared. He no longer felt the exhaustion in his muscles, the ache in his ribs. The ritual had burned those away, leaving only clarity. The shrine's carvings glowed faintly in the firelight, the old stories no longer distant legends but living instructions.

And as the flames roared, he knew: he was not simply a spy in hiding. He was the next participant in a cycle as old as time.

The forest listened. The fire bore witness. The gods watched in silence.

And Kalki was ready.

CHAPTER 5

Into the Fortress

The night had turned colder, the kind of cold that crept under the skin and gnawed at the bones. Mist coiled along the forest floor, moving as though the earth itself exhaled secrets into the dark. Every branch dripped with dew, every shadow seemed deeper than it should.

Kalki and Ananya moved side by side, their steps measured, their silhouettes swallowed by the trees. They did not speak, but the silence between them was not empty—it was heavy with intent. The fire ritual had ended, but its embers still smoldered in Kalki's chest, each heartbeat a reminder of the vow he had made before Agni's witness.

The forest began to thin, the darkness ahead punctured by a faint glow. They crept up a ridge, and from its crest the city revealed itself below.

A sprawl of lights, restless and alive. Cars pulsed along highways like arteries of fire. Towers of glass rose against the mist, their windows glowing with the insomnia of industry. But at the city's edge, looming apart from the sprawl, was their destination.

The fortress.

It was not like the other buildings. Where the city glittered with neon and billboards, the fortress was a block of shadow and steel. A squat tower of black glass, humming with a strange vitality. Around it stretched electrified fences and patrol roads where drones buzzed like hornets. Spotlights cut arcs through the fog, sharp and merciless. Even from a distance, the place radiated menace, as though it were less a structure and more a wound carved into the earth.

Ananya drew her shawl tighter around her shoulders, her breath visible in the cold. "People call it a data fortress," she whispered. "But that name is too small. It isn't just servers and wires. It's... layered. Ritual-like firewalls, logic traps, codes built from mantras. I've glimpsed them. It's like someone wove yajna into machine language."

Kalki's jaw tightened. His eyes stayed fixed on the black tower, his voice low but steady. "Then it isn't just a fortress. It's a Lanka of circuits."

She turned toward him, firelight from the city reflected in her eyes. "Exactly."

The word hung between them, and with it came the weight of memory. Ravana's Lanka—gleaming, impenetrable, a kingdom built on illusion and pride. It had once seemed unassailable too. Until Rama had brought it down with courage, faith, and fire.

Kalki's pulse slowed. This was his battlefield. Tonight, this was Kurukshetra.

"We go in quiet," he said.

They descended the ridge, slipping into the undergrowth. Kalki moved with the ease of habit, each step balanced, each pause timed with the sweep of distant searchlights. He guided Ananya, showing her how to shift her weight to avoid snapping twigs, how to blend into the rhythm of the moving beams. She learned quickly, her fear tempered by determination.

At the perimeter, the fence loomed—tall, coiled with razor wire, alive with current. It was more than a barrier; it was a declaration. *Enter, and die.*

Kalki pressed his palm against the mesh. The metal vibrated with energy, a steady hum that prickled his skin. But beneath the current was something else. Not random. Patterned. A chant hidden in electricity.

He closed his eyes.

1110 0101…ॐ नमः शिवाय…

Binary flickered across his mind, dissolving into Sanskrit syllables, syllables dissolving back into numbers. It was a mantra disguised as machine language, a loop of devotion twisted into defense.

Kalki leaned closer and whispered the mantra back: "ॐ नमः शिवाय."

The hum shifted. The current shivered, faltered, then fell silent. The fence went dead.

Ananya inhaled sharply. "You just—"

"Not me," Kalki said softly, withdrawing his hand. "The network answers when dharma speaks."

They slipped through the gap.

Inside the perimeter, the fortress loomed taller, its black glass reflecting fractured pieces of moonlight. Patrol guards moved in pairs, rifles slung across their shoulders, steps falling in rigid rhythm. Drones hovered overhead, cameras swiveling with insect precision. The air itself seemed thick with surveillance.

Kalki crouched behind a stack of shipping crates, his eyes scanning the patterns. The guards' movements were precise, but patterns always betrayed themselves. He traced their steps in his mind, noting the pause at each intersection, the exact interval of their turns. Twenty-one steps, pause, turn. A cycle of offering, hidden in martial routine.

"We move on the next cycle," he whispered.

Ananya nodded, her breath sharp in the mist.

When the guards turned their backs, Kalki signaled. They darted across open ground, their bodies flowing from shadow to shadow until they pressed against the fortress wall.

A side entrance loomed ahead, seamless black glass with a single red scanner glowing faintly at its center. No handles, no keypad. Only an orb of light that pulsed like a living eye.

Ananya frowned. "Biometric lock. Retinal and fingerprint. We'll need a host to—"

Kalki raised his hand, pressing his palm against the scanner. For a moment, nothing happened. Then symbols flared in his vision. The orb fractured into patterns—Sanskrit verses spiraling through binary knots.

The lock resisted. A serpent of flame coiled within the code, hissing as it wrapped tighter.

But Kalki remembered another serpent. Kāliya, the great naga who had poisoned the Yamunā river, subdued not by weapons but by Krishna's dance. Balance defeating poison.

Kalki whispered: "Om namo bhagavate vāsudevāya."

The serpent writhed, then stilled. The scanner clicked. With a low hiss, the door slid open.

Cold air spilled out, dry and electric.

They stepped inside.

The moment Kalki and Ananya crossed the threshold, the fortress swallowed them whole. The door slid shut behind them with a whisper, sealing off the outside world. Silence reigned, thick and humming, broken only by the low throb of machines.

Rows of servers stretched in every direction, towering pillars of steel and circuitry. Their blinking lights pulsed in hypnotic rhythm, like a thousand heartbeats synced into one. The air was unnaturally dry, laced with ozone and the faint metallic tang of electricity. Even breathing here felt different—heavy, as though the lungs were filling with current instead of air.

Ananya glanced around, awe flickering in her eyes. "It's like… a temple," she whispered. "Not one built for gods, but for something else. Something hungrier."

Kalki said nothing, but he felt it too. The pressure in the air. The weight on his chest. The fortress was alive—not in the way trees or animals lived, but in the way rituals summoned presence. This was not a building; it was a shrine to control.

They moved cautiously between the server rows, their footsteps softened by rubber floors. Overhead, fluorescent lights flickered faintly. At intervals, cameras tracked silently, their lenses glinting red. But each time their gaze seemed to fall upon Kalki, the red lights dimmed, shuddered, and blinked out—like sentinels bowing before something greater.

Ananya's breath quickened. "You're doing that, aren't you?"

Kalki shook his head. "Not me. Dharma."

Her brow furrowed, but she said nothing more.

They pressed deeper. The servers seemed endless, arranged in precise grids that stretched far beyond what the building's exterior should have allowed. The geometry was wrong. Distances stretched. Corridors folded back on themselves. It was as though the fortress was bending space, coiling its innards like the spiral of a *Chakravyuha*.

Kalki's jaw tightened. *Another labyrinth.*

He whispered Krishna's words under his breath:

"You have the right to action alone, never to its fruits."

It steadied him. He was not here to escape the labyrinth—he was here to act within it.

Then the servers flickered.

Screens blinked awake, one after another, rippling down the aisle in a wave. Their glow filled the darkness with pale light. At first they showed static, then code, then symbols. Binary spilled into Sanskrit, Sanskrit twisted into code. And then all of it dissolved into a single image.

A face.

The same face Kalki had glimpsed in the fire ritual. Sharp features, smiling lips, eyes glittering with malice.

Maya.

His voice came through the fortress speakers, smooth and venomous, curling through the air like smoke.

"So," he said. "The avatar comes to my gates. Brave… or foolish?"

Ananya stiffened. Her fingers clutched her shawl tighter. "He can see us."

The screens shifted. Maya's face leaned closer, too close, filling the displays with mocking intimacy. His smile widened.

"You slip through shadows, thinking you are unseen. But I see every breath, every step. Do you think your mantras are hidden from me? I have woven them into my own design. Every chant, every offering—fuel for the network I command."

Kalki stepped forward, unafraid, though every screen followed his movement. His voice was calm, but beneath it burned steel. "You hide behind illusions."

Maya laughed, low and mocking. The sound reverberated in the walls, vibrating through the floor. "Illusion? No. I am illusion. I am *māyā*. Without me, your gods would have no play, no drama, no battlefield for their dharma. I am the dream you call reality. And I can turn dream into nightmare with a single thought."

The screens glitched. Images flickered rapidly—burning cities, rivers of data twisted into black sludge, armies of drones rising like rakshasas, temples collapsing into dust. And woven among them were older visions: Ravana's Lanka aflame, Duryodhana's court drenched in deceit, Bhishma's body pierced with arrows as he lay upon his bed of pain.

Maya's voice slithered through the montage. "You can fight me, Kalki. But every step you take strengthens me. Every verse you whisper feeds my design. Even your dharma is nothing without the illusion I grant it."

The last screen flickered, showing Kalki himself—mud-streaked, bloodied, kneeling before the fire at the shrine. But in this version, his head was bowed not in vow but in defeat. Chains glimmered on his wrists again, as though Maya sought to rewrite his reality.

Ananya reached for his arm, her voice tight. "Don't look. He wants you to believe it."

Kalki did not flinch. His eyes stayed locked on the image. His fists clenched, but his voice was steady. "You know my name," he said quietly. "But you do not know my purpose."

For a moment, the screens froze. Then, as though cut by an unseen hand, they went black. Silence fell.

The only sound was the steady hum of servers, the endless heartbeat of the fortress.

Ananya exhaled shakily, her eyes wide. "He knows who you are. He's already trying to twist it."

Kalki's jaw remained tight, his gaze hard. Inside, the fire of the homam still burned, and it pushed back against the chill of Maya's illusion. "Let him try. Illusion cannot bind what is anchored in dharma."

He turned deeper into the fortress. The servers loomed higher, the corridors stretched longer, and the air thickened with unseen presence. Somewhere ahead, Kalki knew, the true heart of this citadel waited. And with it, the next test.

The servers hummed louder as Kalki and Ananya pressed deeper into the labyrinth. Each row stretched impossibly far, as if space itself were folding in on them. The air grew denser, harder to breathe, saturated with the presence of something watching, something feeding.

Kalki paused at an intersection of server aisles. The floor beneath their feet trembled faintly, a vibration too deliberate to be random. He crouched, pressing his palm to the ground. The rhythm was unmistakable: **108 pulses, pause, repeat.**

Ananya crouched beside him. "It's everywhere," she whispered. "The numbers… they're not patterns in the code anymore. They're in the building itself. It's like the whole fortress is chanting."

Kalki nodded slowly. "Not a fortress. A yajna. A ritual built from steel and circuit."

He stood, scanning the walls. A faint glow traced itself along the edges of the servers—symbols, at first invisible, now shimmering into view. Devanāgarī script danced across the glass panels, interlaced with binary knots. Verses of the Rig Veda bent into firewalls, curling like serpents waiting to strike.

Ananya's eyes widened. "Logic traps," she breathed. "But they're… alive."

A whisper slithered through the air, cold and close. Maya's voice.

"Step forward, avatar. The path is yours to walk. If you are what the stories say, then prove it."

The glow on the servers thickened, rearranging into a lattice across the aisle. Threads of light crisscrossed, forming a barrier of fire and code. The lattice shimmered red and gold, pulsing like veins.

Kalki studied it, his mind parsing what others would see only as chaos. Each strand carried verses, syllables twisted into commands. Together, they formed a **Chakravyuha**—the same formation that had trapped Abhimanyu on Kurukshetra.

Ananya touched his arm, her voice tense. "It's a kill grid. If we cross it wrong, the system will lock every door. We'll be trapped."

Kalki's lips tightened. "Like Abhimanyu."

For a moment, the memory of the young warrior filled him—the courage, the isolation, the fall. But Kalki was no Abhimanyu. He was

Arjuna, and Arjuna had Krishna's counsel. Tonight, he would have to summon that counsel from within.

He inhaled, whispering a mantra. "ॐ नमो भगवते वासुदेवाय."

The lattice responded. One strand flickered, dimming as though bowing. Kalki stepped forward, guiding Ananya carefully. They moved in rhythm—step, breath, mantra. Each cycle dissolved another strand.

But the deeper they went, the more the lattice fought back. Symbols twisted into grotesque shapes, syllables hissing with distortion. Binary writhed like snakes, snapping at their ankles. The verses themselves mocked him, rearranging into cruel taunts:

धर्मम् = illusion
अधर्मम् = truth

Ananya flinched. "It's rewriting meaning—flipping everything."

Maya's laughter filled the aisle. "Dharma, adharma—mere words. I can make them anything I choose. Tell me, Kalki, when your blade spills blood, who decides which word applies?"

The lattice surged, strands lashing outward like whips of fire. Kalki ducked, pulling Ananya close, his knife flashing to cut through a coil of binary. Sparks erupted, searing the air.

He shouted over the hum. "Dharma is not decided by you. Dharma is what stands when illusion burns away."

He stepped forward again, planting his foot firmly. The ground vibrated. Another cycle of 21 pulses passed beneath him, and the lattice weakened. One by one, the strands dissolved, collapsing into ash and code.

Finally, the grid shattered with a hiss, dispersing into sparks that rained down harmlessly. The aisle cleared.

Ananya exhaled, trembling. "You… you treated it like a ritual. The way you timed your steps…"

Kalki nodded once. "It wasn't strength. It was alignment. Every trap has a rhythm. Find it, and you walk free."

Maya's voice slithered back, this time softer, mocking. "Impressive. Perhaps you are worthy of the stories after all. But tell me, avatar—how will you fight an enemy who exists in thought itself? You can cut wires, dodge bullets, whisper mantras into steel. But can you strike an illusion? Can you kill a dream?"

The screens flared again, showing visions—Ananya shackled, her eyes vacant, chanting mantras in endless cycles like the guard Kalki had seen in the prison. Then another vision: Kalki himself, standing over bodies, his hands drenched in blood, temples burning behind him.

Ananya gasped, turning away. "Don't—don't look at it."

But Kalki did look. He stared into the vision of himself, the bloodied reflection Maya thrust at him. And slowly, his jaw tightened.

"You can show me a thousand faces," he said. "But illusion has no weight. Dharma does."

He reached out, and the screen flickered violently, then cracked. Sparks burst. The vision died.

Silence fell again, broken only by the hum of servers.

Kalki turned to Ananya. Her breath came in short bursts, her eyes wide but steady. She had not fled, though fear shook her frame.

"We keep moving," he said.

She nodded, pulling her shawl tighter.

They pressed deeper into the fortress. Ahead, the aisles narrowed, leading toward a central chamber. The hum of the servers grew louder, heavier, until it was not sound but pressure, like the roar of an unseen ocean.

Something vast was waiting there.

The hum of the servers thickened into a roar as they advanced. It was no longer a sound but a vibration that pressed against their bones, rattled their teeth, and made their hearts stumble in rhythm. The air smelled sharp, metallic, like iron left too long in the rain.

The aisle opened into a vast chamber at the fortress's core.

It was circular, its walls lined with towering server racks that curved inward like pillars of some unholy temple. Cables snaked across the floor, thick as roots, pulsing faintly with light. In the center rose a platform of black glass, and above it floated a massive sphere of shifting symbols—binary twisting into Sanskrit, Sanskrit bleeding back into code. It pulsed in cycles, **108 flashes followed by 21 ripples**, as though chanting to itself.

Ananya gasped, her voice trembling. "It's... alive."

Kalki felt it too. The pressure on his chest, the weight on his spirit. This was no machine. This was invocation—ritual transmuted into circuitry, illusion spun into architecture.

The sphere shimmered, and then it broke apart, fragments scattering into the air like shards of a shattered mirror. The pieces rearranged themselves across the walls, forming screens.

And on every screen, his face appeared.

Maya.

The smile was the same—sharp, knowing, cruel. His eyes glowed with a mockery of divinity.

"Welcome," he said, his voice curling through the chamber like smoke. "You have walked my labyrinth, broken my grid, resisted my shadows. Impressive. But now you stand in the sanctum of my design. Here, I am not voice. I am not vision. I am everything."

The screens shifted. Cities burning. Armies marching. Leaders bowing to unseen strings. The world itself flickering as if it were only another projection.

"Do you see?" Maya whispered. "Reality bends to me. Dharma, adharma—they are toys in my hands. Your scriptures spoke of me without naming me. For what is māyā, if not the stage upon which your gods act? Without illusion, your avatars would have no battles to fight. You need me, Kalki. Without me, you are nothing."

The chamber darkened. The screens flared again, this time showing Kalki's face—not as he was, but as Maya wished him to be. Blood smeared his hands. His eyes glowed with fanatic fire. Behind him, temples burned, forests fell, children wept.

"This is you," Maya said. "This is what dharma looks like in my world. Violence clothed in righteousness. Chains disguised as duty."

Ananya cried out, covering her ears. "Stop!"

But the visions only grew stronger. Kalki saw himself crowned in blood, seated upon a throne of weapons. He saw Ananya kneeling, her eyes blank, chanting verses like a broken machine. He saw the fire ritual twisted into sacrifice, the offerings transformed into corpses.

The images pressed against his mind, heavy as chains. His knees trembled. The air thickened. For a heartbeat, he felt the temptation—

to believe it, to surrender, to let Maya define the story.

Then, somewhere deep within him, another voice stirred.

The voice of the battlefield. Krishna's counsel to Arjuna. Rama's silence in exile. Hanuman's laughter as fire consumed Lanka.

Dharma was not image. Not illusion. Not what others named it. Dharma was action, born of clarity.

Kalki inhaled sharply. His chest burned, not with Maya's pressure but with the ember that had never died since the shrine. He whispered, steady and fierce:

"Yato dharmas tato jayah."

Where there is dharma, there is victory.

The words struck the chamber like a bell. The visions flickered, faltered. The crown of blood dissolved, the burning temples dimmed, the false Ananya vanished.

The screens glitched violently, Maya's smile shattering into static. His voice rose, sharper now, tinged with anger. "You think a mantra can undo me? Fool. Every syllable you speak strengthens my network. Every verse you whisper feeds my design!"

Kalki stepped forward, his fists clenched. "Then let it feed. Let every syllable become fire. And when the fire burns through illusion, only dharma will remain."

The servers screamed, lights strobing wildly, as though the fortress itself recoiled. The sphere above the platform pulsed erratically, its cycle breaking, its rhythm faltering.

Ananya grasped his arm, eyes wide with awe and fear. "You shook him. Do you realize what you just did?"

Kalki's gaze stayed on the trembling sphere. "Not enough. This is only the beginning."

The chamber groaned, cables rattling, alarms shrieking in protest. The fortress trembled as though Maya himself writhed within its circuits.

But Kalki stood steady. In the chaos, he felt clarity. Maya had revealed his strength—and his weakness. He thrived on illusion, but illusion could not withstand fire.

Kalki raised his hand toward the sphere. His voice was calm, his vow unshaken.

"Your stage is wide, Maya. But dharma has no walls. I will walk every labyrinth you build. I will break every illusion you weave. And when the cycle ends, it is not you the world will remember."

The sphere convulsed once more, then dimmed, its hum subsiding into a low growl. The screens flickered, Maya's smile returning—smaller now, colder, more calculating.

"You are not ready," he hissed. "But you will be. And when you fall, Kalki, it will be by your own hand."

The screens went black. The fortress fell into silence, save for the distant thrum of servers, subdued and restless.

Ananya exhaled, her hands trembling. "We should leave before it resets."

Kalki turned from the sphere, his face calm though his blood still burned. "Yes. But we will return. This is not the end. Only the first strike."

Together, they slipped back into the labyrinth, shadows moving through shadows. Behind them, the fortress hummed like a wounded beast, and somewhere in its depths, Maya smiled still.

CHAPTER 6

The First Fragment

The fortress swallowed sound as they moved deeper inside. Every footstep seemed to vanish into the thick air, muffled by the hum of servers that rose around them like black monoliths. Their blinking lights pulsed steadily, a rhythm too precise to be random—like the measured beat of a colossal heart.

Kalki led the way, body angled low, every muscle attuned to shadow and sound. His knife glinted faintly at his belt, though his true weapons were his eyes, scanning every reflection, every flicker. Ananya followed close behind, clutching the small pack strapped across her shoulder. Her fingers twitched at her sides, eager to reach the device within, but she forced them still, matching her breath to his pace.

They came at last to a chamber unlike the sterile halls they had crossed. The walls were sheathed in mirrored panels that caught and multiplied the faint light. A single console pulsed in the center, glowing with a cold, steady blue.

Even before stepping inside, Kalki felt the shift. The air was heavier here, dense with presence. He raised his hand, motioning Ananya to wait, and entered first.

The mirrors caught him instantly.

At first they reflected what he expected: a man bruised, mud-streaked, his face drawn from battle and exhaustion. But then, the reflection shifted. His hair darkened, his skin gleamed under black armor, and his eyes blazed red with unnatural fire. A sword hung in his grip, dripping with fresh blood.

Kalki staggered back, breath quickening. His hand went instinctively to his knife.

From the mirror came a whisper in his own voice, but twisted, heavy with venom:

"You are no savior. You are Duryodhana reborn. A tyrant in waiting."

The words clawed at him. For a heartbeat he felt the weight of them—how easy it would be for strength to curdle into tyranny, for dharma to become justification for cruelty.

Ananya's hand caught his arm, grounding him. "Don't look too long," she said quickly. Her voice was steady, but her grip trembled. "It's a projection. An Indrajit illusion. Maya knows your doubts."

But the mirrors did not stop. Another panel flared to life, and this time the vision pierced deeper.

Sītā.

She stood bound among dark trees, her face pale, her eyes hollow with despair. The sorrow in her gaze struck Kalki's chest like an arrow. He could almost hear the faint weeping, the ache of exile and captivity.

"You cannot save them all," the mirror hissed. "You could not save her. You will fail again."

Kalki shut his eyes. His breath faltered. The vision reached into his deepest fear—not death, not defeat, but failure to protect. Failure to honor dharma.

This is Kurukshetra, he reminded himself. *This is Arjuna, frozen with despair, unable to lift his bow.*

And then, from memory's depths, Krishna's voice rose like a conch call:

"The self is not slain when the body is slain. Do your duty, O Arjuna."

Kalki exhaled sharply. His chest steadied. He opened his eyes—not to the illusions, but through them.

The mirrors shivered. Cracks split across their surfaces, spiderwebbing outward until the panels shattered silently, fragments falling inward and dissolving before they touched the ground.

The chamber cleared. The visions vanished. Only the console remained, glowing faintly in the center like a solitary star.

Ananya released her grip on his arm. Her face was pale, but her eyes burned with determination. She moved to the console, her fingers already pulling the device from her pack.

"This isn't just a terminal," she whispered. "It's a gateway."

She knelt, connecting the device with swift, practiced motions. The console flared, its screen blooming with cascading code. But the code was not code alone. Binary threads wove into Sanskrit slokas, the verses bending and twisting like vines. The language of machines merged with the language of prayer.

Ananya's brow furrowed as she worked, her fingers flying across the interface. Lines of symbols danced across the screen—familiar yet broken, sacred yet corrupted.

Finally, a block of script glowed crimson. Half-verse, half-error.

धर्मो रक्षति रक्षितः... 0110101... ERROR ERROR...

Kalki leaned closer, reading the fractured words aloud. "*Dharmo rakṣati rakṣitaḥ.* Dharma protects those who protect it."

But even as he spoke, the line broke, splintered by binary corruption, the syllables twisted out of truth.

Ananya's face drained of color. "This is it. The first fragment."

She touched the screen lightly, her voice dropping. "It's rewriting dharma itself. Whoever controls this can bend morality—make any atrocity seem righteous, twist truth into illusion."

Kalki's fists tightened at his sides. The weight of it was worse than theft, worse than destruction. This was corruption of the very foundation upon which action was judged. If dharma itself could be rewritten, the world would fall into chaos without knowing it had fallen.

He looked at Ananya. "We can't let it remain here."

Her lips pressed into a thin line. "No. But carrying it makes us targets. Maya will not allow this to leave without cost."

The console's glow deepened, shifting from faint blue to a throbbing crimson. The mirrored shards on the floor dissolved into mist, curling upward and vanishing into the air. The servers lining the chamber hummed louder, their blinking lights stuttering in uneven rhythm, as though agitated.

Ananya's fingers moved in a blur across her interface, trying to stabilize the connection. Lines of code spilled across the display—binary streams colliding with Sanskrit hymns, verses mutating into error messages.

"It's fighting me," she muttered. "The system isn't just protected—it's alive. Every time I touch the code, it reweaves itself. Like it knows I'm here."

Kalki's eyes never left the mirrored walls. Though shattered, they pulsed faintly, their silver surfaces rippling as though breath passed beneath them. His reflection appeared again for the briefest instant—his own face, bloodied and beaten. Then it warped, showing him crowned, armored, sitting upon a throne of ash. His jaw tightened.

Ananya hissed, pulling him back to focus. "Kalki! Look."

On the console, a block of script surged forward, glowing brighter than the rest. It pulsed like a living heart. Half of it was verse, half corrupted static:

धर्मो रक्षति रक्षितः // 01100101 01110010 01110010 — ERROR — ERROR

The verse fractured midstream, its sacred meaning bleeding into nonsense.

Ananya's voice was tight. "This is the fragment. The *first fragment.* Maya's anchor point."

Kalki leaned closer. The glow of the text painted his skin red, like firelight. "Anchor point?"

She nodded. "Think of the Network like a body. This fragment is not just data—it's a *nerve cluster.* Whoever holds it can send signals that define morality itself. They can make nations believe slaughter is justice, tyranny is protection. It's like... rewriting the conscience of the world."

Kalki's chest tightened. He thought of Arjuna again, bow slipping from his hand as he faced kin across the battlefield. Despair. Paralysis. And Krishna's counsel:

"Your right is to action alone. Do not be attached to results."

But what if the very definition of right could be rewritten? What if illusion itself could become dharma in the minds of men?

The thought chilled him more than any weapon.

Before he could answer, the chamber shuddered. The servers roared, fans screaming like beasts roused from slumber. The mirrored walls rippled wildly, no longer reflections but pools of liquid shadow.

Maya's voice poured from the speakers—smooth, calm, and venomous.

"Ah," he whispered. "You've found it. My little gift."

Ananya froze, her hands suspended above the console. Her face paled.

Maya chuckled softly, the sound slithering across the chamber. "Go on. Take it. Take the fragment, Kalki. Carry it into the world. Every righteous act you attempt will ripple through my code. Every verse you whisper, every prayer you chant, will feed my design. You will be my courier, my messenger. You will spread me without knowing it."

The mirrored walls came alive with images—battlefields burning, temples collapsing, rivers of soldiers marching with blank eyes. In every reflection, Kalki stood at the center, his knife dripping blood, his hands raised in command.

"You will be remembered not as savior," Maya hissed, "but as the tyrant you secretly fear."

Ananya reached instinctively for his arm, her voice sharp. "Don't listen! It's bait."

Kalki's fists clenched, but his gaze did not falter. "You're trying to chain me with doubt."

Maya's laugh rolled through the chamber. "Doubt is the truest chain, avatar. Stronger than steel, sharper than fire. Why do you think Arjuna froze before his own kin? Why did Rama wander the forest when his throne was stolen? Doubt. Doubt makes heroes useful to me."

The console flared suddenly, the pulsing script coalescing into form. A crystalline shard of light rose from the interface, spinning slowly. Its surface shimmered with shifting mantras, each one corrupted, rewritten, poisoned.

Ananya inhaled sharply. "The fragment… it's solidifying."

She reached forward, slipping it into a shielded capsule from her pack. The crystal resisted at first, vibrating violently, but with a final spark it settled, its glow dimmed by containment.

The servers dimmed in response. The mirrored walls dulled, their visions receding. For a moment, silence returned to the chamber.

Kalki turned toward the shadows, voice steady. "You think I will carry your poison willingly. But dharma burns away corruption. Even your illusions cannot withstand fire."

Maya's voice softened, almost a whisper. "We shall see."

The mirrors stilled. The servers calmed. The room fell quiet again.

Ananya clutched the capsule close to her chest. Her face was pale, but her jaw was set. "We can't destroy it here. We need to study it, find its source."

Kalki nodded slowly. His gaze swept the chamber one last time, searching for any lingering shadow. Then he adjusted the strap of his knife, his expression hard.

"Then we move. Kurukshetra was never won by hesitation."

The capsule pulsed faintly in Ananya's hands, its surface vibrating with a rhythm that was not her own. She tightened her grip on it, tucking it carefully into the shielded pouch at her side. Even through the layers of fabric and alloy, the fragment seemed to hum against her ribs, as though whispering.

Kalki kept his eyes on the darkened mirrors, his knife loose but ready in his hand. He knew better than to believe silence meant safety. Maya had withdrawn his voice, but that absence was not mercy. It was calculation.

"Stay close," he said quietly.

They slipped back into the fortress corridors. The servers hummed again, their lights flickering in odd patterns. What had once seemed orderly now glitched, blinking in sequences of **21 red flashes, then 108 green**—a rhythm repeating like a heartbeat.

Ananya noticed it too. "It's… watching us," she whispered. "It's aligning itself to our steps."

Kalki's jaw tightened. "Then we move against the rhythm. Never let illusion dictate pace."

He altered his stride, pausing unpredictably, turning at irregular intervals. The flickers faltered, stuttering as if the fortress itself grew frustrated.

But soon, resistance came.

A faint buzz rose in the air. Shadows moved above them. Drones slipped from the ceiling, black and sleek, their lenses glowing with crimson light. They spread out in precise formation, wings whirring, each armed with tranquilizer rifles.

Ananya froze, her breath catching. "We can't fight all of them."

Kalki's eyes flicked across the formation. He didn't need to fight them all. He needed only to break the rhythm.

The drones circled, their movements in perfect synchrony: **twenty-one rotations around the chamber, then a pause**. He crouched, watching carefully. On the twenty-first cycle, their wings slowed, just for a heartbeat.

"Now," he whispered.

He leapt forward, his knife flashing. One drone fell with a sputter of sparks. He kicked its body into another, the collision shorting both.

The others whirled, beams converging on him. But in that instant, Ananya raised her device, fingers racing. Her screen blazed with Sanskrit and code, her voice muttering: "ॐ अग्रेय नमः… Override protocol—"

The drones faltered midair, their lights flickering. For a moment, they hovered aimlessly, like puppets with severed strings. Then two collapsed, smashing into the floor.

Kalki spun, slicing the last as it swooped. It shattered against the ground in a shower of sparks. Silence returned, sharp and sudden.

Ananya exhaled shakily, lowering her device. "That was too close."

Kalki crouched beside the fallen drones, scanning their designs. Inscribed faintly along their frames were Sanskrit syllables—carved, not coded. He traced them with his finger.

"Mantras etched into metal," he murmured. "Maya isn't just embedding illusion in circuits. He's binding it into matter itself."

Ananya shuddered. "Then the fortress isn't just built with technology. It's consecrated."

They moved again, deeper into the labyrinth. The corridors grew narrower, twisting. The servers pulsed louder, their lights bending into strange shapes. At first they seemed like patterns of code. Then faces. Then whole scenes.

Kalki slowed. Along the walls, images played out in cascading sequences—reflections of his life, but twisted. He saw himself as a child, kneeling before the temple fire. Then the image shifted—he was older, his knife in hand, plunging it into his guru's chest.

He clenched his teeth. "Illusion."

The scene shifted again—Ananya at the shrine, chanting, her eyes vacant, her hands covered in blood.

Ananya gasped, stepping back. "No—"

Kalki grabbed her wrist firmly. "Look through it, not at it. Illusion cannot wound unless you accept it."

The images cracked, dissolving into static. The corridor cleared, leaving only the endless hum of servers.

Ananya steadied her breath, her face pale. "He's trying to wear us down. Break us with fear."

Kalki's gaze was cold. "Fear is his weapon. But dharma burns fear away."

They reached another checkpoint—thick doors of reinforced steel, glowing faintly with inscriptions. Sanskrit syllables looped across their surface, alternating with binary. **108 glyphs, 21 locks.**

Ananya's hands hovered over her device. "It'll take time—"

Kalki shook his head. "Time is illusion. Rhythm is truth."

He pressed his palm to the door. At once, symbols surged into his mind's eye, a lattice of fire and code. Snakes of corrupted mantra snapped at him, hissing static. He whispered calmly:

"ॐ नमो भगवते वासुदेवाय."

Each repetition aligned with a lock. **108 chants.** Slowly, one by one, the seals broke. With a final hiss, the door groaned open.

Beyond lay the outer corridors, faint light spilling from the exit.

Ananya looked at him with awe. "How did you—"

"Because dharma doesn't beg entry," he said softly. "It walks where it must."

They stepped into the final hall. The capsule at Ananya's side pulsed brighter, as though straining to be free. Behind them, the fortress trembled, servers humming with anger.

And then Maya's voice returned, deeper than before, resonant through the walls.

"You carry my heart now, Kalki. You cannot destroy it. You cannot even escape it. You think you walk for dharma, but every step serves me."

The corridor shook violently. Lights burst overhead, raining sparks.

Kalki tightened his grip on the knife. His voice was steady, cutting through the chaos:

"You name yourself illusion. Then you should know: fire reveals truth. And I carry fire in my veins."

The corridor convulsed as though the fortress itself were alive, its walls rippling, metal groaning under unseen strain. Sparks rained from the ceiling, smoke curling upward in pale streams. The fragment pulsed violently inside Ananya's pack, each beat echoing like a drum against their chests.

"Run," Kalki ordered.

They sprinted down the narrowing hall, their footsteps pounding in rhythm with the fragment's pulse. Behind them, the servers shrieked, their lights strobing in seizure—**21 bursts of red, 108 of white**—a final chant of resistance.

Ahead, the exit doors loomed, but even as they neared, the floor beneath them rippled like water. The ground split into jagged fissures, and out of the cracks rose shadows—figures sculpted from static and smoke. They marched in formation, faceless, armored, their hands clutching rifles of pure code.

Ananya gasped. "They're not real—"

"They're real enough to stop us."

The phantoms advanced. Their boots struck in unison, each step echoing like a war drum. In their silence Kalki heard the memory of Kurukshetra—the massing of armies, the trembling of earth under countless hooves.

For a moment, despair threatened him again. But then, he remembered: this was no different from Arjuna staring at his kin across the battlefield. Illusion, no matter how vast, was still illusion.

Kalki stepped forward, his voice rising in steady mantra:

"ॐ अग्नये स्वाहा..."

The air rippled. Fire licked at the fissures, sparks flaring at his feet. The shadows faltered, their edges fraying under the heat.

He advanced another step, chanting louder:

"ॐ नमो भगवते वासुदेवाय."

The shadows hissed, writhing like serpents struck by flame. Their rifles dissolved into static. One by one, they collapsed back into smoke, sucked into the cracks from which they had risen.

The fissures sealed. The floor solidified. The hall cleared.

Ananya's eyes shone with awe. "You... burned them away."

Kalki's voice was calm, but firm. "Fire reveals truth. It always has."

They reached the doors. Another set of biometric locks glowed across the steel—fingerprint, retina, code. But the fortress was weakening. When Kalki pressed his palm against the scanner, the glyphs barely resisted. The locks clicked open in rapid sequence, like soldiers saluting in surrender.

With a final groan, the doors slid apart.

Cool night air swept over them, carrying the smell of wet earth and pine. Mist rolled in thick waves, and stars shimmered faintly above the city's haze. For a heartbeat, the silence felt pure, untouched.

But then, Maya's voice followed them, whispering through the mist.

"You think you have won a fragment. But fragments are pieces of a whole. Carry it, avatar. Protect it. Fear it. Every step you take will lead you deeper into my design. You are already woven into me."

The mist thickened. For a moment, it shaped itself into a face—Maya's sharp features, his cruel smile—before dispersing into the night.

Ananya clutched the capsule tighter against her chest. Her lips trembled, but her eyes hardened. "We can't keep this forever. If even one fragment holds this much power…"

Kalki looked out into the forest, its shadows deep, its silence vast. His body ached, his lungs burned, but within his chest the ember still glowed. He thought of the shrine, the fire, the vow he had made before the carvings of Rama and Krishna.

He turned to her, his voice steady. "We won't keep it. We'll learn it. Understand it. And then we'll burn every illusion it carries."

His gaze shifted to the stars, their cold fire watching like ancient eyes.

"Kurukshetra isn't behind us," he said quietly. "It's ahead. This was only the first strike."

They descended into the mist-draped forest, the capsule's glow faint through Ananya's pack. Behind them, the fortress pulsed once, a final heartbeat of defiance, before falling dark.

And somewhere, unseen, Maya smiled.

CHAPTER 7

The Chakravyuha Trap

The corridors of the fortress stretched endlessly before them, longer and darker than when they had first come. Every step echoed too loudly, rebounding down steel walls that seemed to lean inward as though listening.

Kalki's instincts screamed. Something in the air had shifted. The servers no longer hummed in rhythm—they pulsed erratically, as if agitated. A faint vibration rolled through the floor, not mechanical but alive, like a sleeping beast stirred awake.

Ananya walked a half-step behind him, one hand clutching the strap of her pack where the capsule lay hidden. She could feel its warmth even through the fabric, a faint pulse against her ribs. Her breath came quick, shallow.

"Something's wrong," she whispered. "The walls… they're watching."

Kalki nodded once. His knife brushed lightly against his palm, ready. "He won't let us leave so easily."

They turned the corner—and froze.

The passageway had changed. Where there should have been a straight hall leading to the perimeter, the corridor now split into three branching paths, each one identical: polished steel, mirrored racks of servers, glowing lines of red light at the edges. The symmetry was unnerving. The air itself seemed to thrum with repetition.

Ananya's eyes darted left, then right. Her voice caught in her throat. "This isn't architecture."

"No," Kalki murmured. "It's a formation."

The word awoke an old memory. He was a boy again, sitting cross-legged by a temple fire, listening to an old priest with a voice like gravel recounting tales of Kurukshetra. The chakravyuha. The spiral formation taught by Drona, impenetrable and merciless. Few could enter, fewer still could escape. Abhimanyu, son of Arjuna, had pierced it bravely—but trapped within, surrounded by masters, he had fallen before his time.

Kalki's jaw clenched. He felt the weight of the boy's sacrifice echoing across centuries. *History will not repeat itself.*

He stepped into the center path. The air thickened immediately, the hum of the servers deepening into a low chant. Ananya followed, her eyes wide, her breath quick.

The fortress shifted with them. Corridors bent unnaturally, folding back on themselves. Lights blinked not randomly, but in strict patterns—**108 flashes, then 21 dark beats** before the cycle resumed. The very building had become a mantra, repeating itself endlessly.

Ananya swallowed hard. "It's chanting. The whole fortress."

Kalki didn't answer. His shoulders were taut, every sense alert. He could feel it now—the tightening spiral, the walls pressing closer, the trap closing like jaws.

A high whine cut through the air. Drones emerged from ceiling alcoves, one after another, their rotors buzzing like angry wasps. Their lenses glowed red, eyes of hunger. They moved in formation—**twenty-one in all**—their circular pattern echoing the trap's design.

Gunfire cracked. Hidden panels in the walls slid open, and guards poured out, rifles raised. Their boots struck the floor in unison, their formation too precise, too disciplined to be coincidence.

The chakravyuha had come alive.

Bullets screamed across the corridor. Kalki shoved Ananya down, rolling forward as steel splinters exploded around them. He grabbed the ankle of the first guard, yanking hard. The man toppled, rifle clattering across the floor. Kalki snatched it mid-spin, firing two bursts that cut down the next pair.

The drones descended, their muzzles glowing. Red beams sprayed the hall. Kalki rolled behind a console, pulling Ananya with him as sparks showered.

"They're herding us," she gasped. "Pushing us deeper."

Kalki's breath was steady, his eyes cold. "That's what a chakravyuha does. It forces you forward. Until there's no way out."

Ananya's hands trembled as she pulled her device from her pack. Her voice was quick, desperate. "I can jam the drones for thirty seconds—no more."

"Do it," he barked, firing controlled bursts. Each shot was deliberate, precise. He didn't waste bullets. Every movement was prayer.

Ananya's fingers flew across her interface, code cascading. Sanskrit merged with binary on her screen:

108 lines of override. 21 failsafes bypassed.

She whispered mantras under her breath as she typed, her voice merging with the rhythm of the code. The drones faltered, their lights flickering erratically. Two crashed into the wall, shattering in sparks. Another spiraled into the ground, wings snapping.

But the relief was short-lived. New drones slid from the ceiling, their rotors sharper, their movements faster. The fortress was adapting.

The circle was tightening.

Kalki fired again, but more guards emerged, each wave stronger than the last. The formation pressed closer, walls bending inward, drones circling above.

He remembered Abhimanyu's last stand—surrounded, lion-hearted, but crushed by numbers.

He inhaled slowly. *Not this time.*

Gunfire cracked like thunder in the steel corridors. Sparks rained from the walls where bullets struck, ricocheting in bursts of white light. The air filled with the stench of ozone and the metallic tang of blood.

Kalki moved like water, every shift of his body calculated, flowing from strike to strike. He ducked under the sweep of a rifle butt, drove his elbow into a guard's ribs, twisted the man's weapon free, and used it to strike another across the jaw. His movements were not just fighting—they were rhythm, action flowing into action like verses into a mantra.

But for every guard he felled, two more surged forward. They were not fighting as men; they were fighting as parts of the formation.

The **Chakravyuha tightened.**

Above, the drones swarmed in concentric circles, their wings slicing the air in a relentless hum. They fired in precise bursts: **twenty-one rounds each, then pause, then resume.** Even their violence was ritualized.

Kalki ducked behind a server bank, his chest heaving. Beside him, Ananya crouched, her device pressed against her knees. Her fingers trembled, her breath coming in sharp gasps.

"They've coded the drones to rotate in cycles," she said quickly, her voice thin but steady. "108 seconds of fire, then 21 of recharge. That's the only window."

Kalki's eyes narrowed. "Then we move on the pause."

But the fortress wasn't waiting. The floor shifted beneath them, rippling like liquid. The walls stretched taller, their mirrored surfaces flickering with light. Reflections of Kalki and Ananya multiplied endlessly, bending into grotesque distortions.

In one reflection, Kalki stood blood-drenched, his knife dripping as Ananya lay lifeless at his feet. In another, he wore Ravana's ten heads, laughing as flames devoured cities. In yet another, he saw Abhimanyu, boy-faced and brave, standing alone as spears pierced him from every side.

The reflections whispered together, voices weaving into one:

"You cannot escape the circle. You are no Kalki. You are Abhimanyu, doomed to die within the spiral."

Ananya clutched his arm, her eyes darting to the reflections. "Don't listen. They're feeding on your memory."

But the words dug deep. Kalki felt the pull of history, the cycle repeating. His breath quickened, his hand tightened on the rifle. *Am I just another sacrifice? Another pawn in the war?*

He closed his eyes. In the chaos, in the storm, he searched inward. And in the silence of his heart, he remembered Krishna's voice, carried across time:

"He who sees inaction in action, and action in inaction, is wise. He alone is a yogi, a warrior of truth."

His chest steadied. The reflections wavered. The whispers faltered.

Kalki opened his eyes, fire burning in them. "I am not Abhimanyu," he said, voice ringing through the corridor. "I carry more than half the memory. I carry the way out."

He rose.

The drones paused, their 108-second cycle ending. For 21 beats, their wings slowed. Kalki surged forward, firing in precise bursts, each shot finding its mark. One drone spiraled down in smoke. Another exploded in a burst of sparks.

Ananya raised her device, voice sharp with mantra: "ॐ अग्नये स्वाहा!"

The screen flared. A pulse of code radiated outward, striking the drones. Five dropped at once, their wings locking, their bodies slamming into the ground like stones.

The guards rushed, shouting, their boots pounding in unison. Kalki met them head-on. He swung the rifle like a staff, knocking one flat, kicking another into the wall. His knife flashed, slicing wires that tethered a drone to the ceiling. Sparks rained down like fireflies.

Still, the walls closed tighter. The corridors bent inward, folding into a spiral. The **Chakravyuha was alive.**

Kalki's breath was steady, but his muscles burned. Sweat stung his eyes. He knew he could not fight forever. The circle was not meant to be broken by force.

He dropped into a crouch, pressing his palm against the floor. Beneath the steel, he felt the pulse—the rhythm of the fortress itself. It was not chaos. It was a mantra.

108 pulses, then 21. Again and again.

He whispered under his breath, syncing his voice with the beat. "ॐ नमो भगवते वासुदेवाय."

The fortress shivered. The spiral wavered. For the briefest moment, a line of light split the wall ahead—an opening.

Kalki stood, pulling Ananya with him. "There. That's the path."

She looked up, her eyes wide. "How did you—"

"No time. Run."

They sprinted, weaving through fire and smoke. The drones shrieked overhead, bullets tearing the air. Guards shouted behind them, their boots thundering in pursuit. The spiral walls bent and twisted, trying to close, but the path held—thin, fragile, but clear.

At its end, faint light gleamed. The exit.

The exit gleamed faintly ahead, a thin line of silver light at the end of the spiral. But every step they took, the fortress fought harder.

The walls groaned, steel bending like clay. The spiral tightened, its arcs folding inward until the corridor became a narrowing throat. Above, the drones swarmed again, their lenses burning like red suns. From the walls, fresh panels slid open, disgorging more guards in precise, timed bursts—**21 at a time**, each wave more disciplined than the last.

Kalki's breath was steady, but his pulse hammered in his ears. He fired short, precise bursts, never wasting a shot. Ananya crouched low behind him, her device in hand, firing off pulses of override code. Sparks spat from the drones overhead as half a dozen dropped, their wings locking midair.

But for every one destroyed, two more emerged. The spiral was endless.

And then Maya's voice filled the corridor.

"Abhimanyu," he whispered, smooth as oil. "Do you think the story will end differently this time?"

The walls lit up.

On every mirrored surface, Kalki saw visions of Kurukshetra: the young prince Abhimanyu, alone in the spiral, his bow snapping under the weight of enemies. He saw spears thrust into the boy's chest, saw blood soaking the earth, saw his body fall beneath countless boots.

The vision shifted. The boy's face melted into his own. Kalki's reflection staggered under the same blows, arrows piercing his skin, spears driving him to his knees.

"You know the ending," Maya whispered. "You enter, you fight, you fall. Dharma dies with you."

Ananya grabbed his arm. "Don't look at it!"

But the vision pressed harder. Another mirror flared: Rama, watching helplessly as Sītā was stolen by Ravana. Another: Krishna, mocked in Duryodhana's court as dharma itself was bound and beaten.

The voices rose, weaving into a chant:

"You cannot save them.
You cannot save her.
You cannot save yourself."

Kalki shut his eyes. For a heartbeat, despair clawed at him, cold and sharp. He felt Abhimanyu's loneliness, Rama's grief, Krishna's silence. He felt the trap tightening not around his body, but his soul.

And then—he remembered the fire.

The ritual at the ruined shrine. The vow he had made before Agni, before the carvings of Rama, Krishna, and Hanuman. He remembered the words that had burned into him:

"Yato dharmas tato jayah.Where there is dharma, there is victory."

His chest filled with heat. The ember flared.

Kalki opened his eyes. The mirrors still showed him pierced, broken, defeated. But now he saw something else: the illusion itself trembling at the edges.

He planted his feet firmly, his voice rising steady, fierce, unshaken:

"ॐ नमो भगवते वासुदेवाय."

The walls shook. The spiral cracked.

He repeated it again, louder:

"ॐ नमो भगवते वासुदेवाय!"

The drones faltered midair. Guards stumbled, their rifles trembling in their hands. The mirrors split, spiderwebbing across their surfaces.

Ananya stared, her eyes wide. The resonance of his mantra wasn't just sound—it was alignment. His voice synced with the fortress's pulse, cutting through its cycle of **108 and 21**, breaking its rhythm, unraveling its coherence.

The spiral screamed. Metal twisted violently. Sparks exploded from the servers. The entire corridor convulsed as though the fortress itself were in pain.

Maya's voice rose, sharp now, almost desperate. "You cannot break what you are inside! You *are* the circle! You are Abhimanyu's death!"

Kalki bellowed the mantra one final time, each syllable a hammer blow:

"ॐ नमो भगवते वासुदेवाय!"

The fortress shattered.

The spiral dissolved into streams of light, the corridors flattening, realigning. For a heartbeat, all was white brilliance, like the flare of a thousand suns. Then silence.

When the glow cleared, the corridor was straight again. Ahead, the exit door loomed, glowing faintly as if touched by divine hand. The drones were gone. The guards had vanished. Only wreckage remained, smoking on the floor.

Ananya gasped, her shoulders shaking. "You… you broke it. You broke the chakravyuha."

Kalki's chest heaved, but his gaze was steady. "Abhimanyu knew the way in. I carry both halves—the entrance and the exit. The memory is complete."

The capsule pulsed in her pack, faint but insistent, as if echoing his words.

Behind them, the fortress groaned like a wounded beast. But the path forward was open.

"Run," Kalki said.

And together, they sprinted toward the light.

The exit door loomed ahead, its steel surface glowing faintly as though lit from within. Each step toward it felt like running through the aftermath of a battle—smoke, sparks, and the acrid stench of burnt circuitry filled the air.

Kalki's body ached, his ribs throbbing from close calls, his palms raw from gripping rifle and blade. But his stride never faltered. Behind him, Ananya pressed close, clutching her pack to her chest as though it were a heart that might break if she let it slip. Inside, the capsule pulsed faintly, each beat syncing with her own.

The corridor shook violently. A roar rose from the depths of the fortress, metallic and guttural, as though the building itself were alive and enraged. Panels blew free from the walls, crashing to the floor. Lights exploded overhead.

And then Maya's voice returned, deeper, sharper, each word a blade.

"You think you broke my circle? Fool. The chakravyuha does not break. It bends. It reforms. It waits. Even your victory is mine."

The walls rippled again, faint shapes flickering across them—Kalki kneeling in chains, Ananya blindfolded, the capsule cracked open and leaking darkness into the earth. For a heartbeat, the vision pressed hard, trying to force itself upon their minds.

Kalki didn't slow. He pressed his palm against the exit scanner. The glyphs that had resisted before now yielded easily, their 108 locks opening in quick sequence, as if bowing to the rhythm of his mantra.

The doors groaned, then slid wide.

Cool night air swept over them, cutting through the heat and smoke. Mist rolled across the ground, thick and pale, swallowing the forest beyond. The alarms of the fortress howled behind them, red lights pulsing like the beat of an enraged heart.

They stepped into the open.

Ananya bent double, gasping, her hands trembling as she clutched the pack. Her voice broke between breaths. "How... how did you do it? The chakravyuha—it wasn't supposed to be possible."

Kalki stared back at the fortress. Its black glass glowed faintly red, like an ember refusing to die. His eyes were dark, but steady. "Abhimanyu carried only half the memory. He knew how to enter. He did not know how to break it. I carry both. The Network showed me."

Ananya straightened slowly, shivering in the mist. She pulled the pack tighter, her voice low. "Maya won't stop now. Not after this. We're not just intruders anymore. We're threats."

Kalki's lips curved into the faintest trace of a smile—not joy, but resolve. "Good. Let him see us as threats. Fear sharpens the edge of dharma."

Behind them, the fortress roared one last time, its alarms shrieking into the night. But the walls did not reform. The circle did not close. For the first time, the chakravyuha had been broken by one who walked out alive.

Kalki turned away, his steps slow but sure. The mist swallowed his silhouette as he spoke, voice low but fierce, a vow carried into the night:

"This war will not end as it began. Illusion will not decide its story. I will."

Ananya followed, her pack glowing faintly at her side. The fragment pulsed within, like a heartbeat—or a ticking clock.

The forest waited, its silence deep, its shadows endless. The battlefield was not behind them. It was ahead.

And Maya, watching from the circuits of the world, smiled in the dark.

CHAPTER 8

Shadows Over the City

The train slid into the city under cover of night, its windows streaked with rain. The wheels clattered on the tracks in a rhythm that seemed almost deliberate—**108 beats before a pause, 21 before resuming.** To most passengers it was noise. To Kalki, it was a warning.

He sat near the rear, hood pulled low, eyes fixed on the reflection in the glass. The faint light from the carriage ceiling painted his face in fragments—half shadow, half fire. Across from him sat Ananya, her hands folded protectively around the pack on her lap. Inside, the capsule pulsed faintly, its glow hidden from the others but felt by both of them like a second heartbeat.

The skyline rose ahead, jagged towers piercing the mist. Neon bled weakly against the storm, advertising gods and machines with the same weary glow. It looked alive, yet sickly, like a titan coughing blood.

"You shouldn't have come back here," Ananya murmured. Her voice was tight, frayed at the edges. "Maya will know. He'll see everything through the grid."

"He already sees," Kalki said quietly. His gaze stayed on the reflection in the glass. "The question is, how much will he burn to stop us?"

The train slowed, brakes squealing in protest. A gust of damp air swept in as the doors hissed open. The city's pulse greeted them immediately—honking horns above, buzzing lights, the restless chatter of midnight streets.

They stepped onto the platform, lost among weary commuters. For a moment, it seemed normal. Just another night in a city that never slept.

Then the lights went out.

It began with the station. Fluorescent lamps flickered once, twice, then died, plunging the platform into shadow. A heartbeat later, the blackout surged upward—streetlamps extinguished, traffic lights dead, neon signs dissolving into darkness.

Aboveground, chaos erupted. Cars screeched to a halt, smashing into one another in intersections. Sirens wailed as transformers blew, showering sparks onto the asphalt. The air filled with panicked voices, shouting, colliding, stumbling in the dark.

Ananya clutched Kalki's arm, her eyes wide. "It's him. He's hijacking the grid."

Kalki's gaze swept the smoke-filled street. Shadows shifted where none should move. People staggered blindly, some trampled in the crush. A transformer exploded, sending orange fire curling upward.

And then, above the city, a single drone descended. Larger than the ones they had faced in the fortress, its body gleamed like polished obsidian. A crimson lens pulsed at its center. Its speakers crackled to life, and a voice poured down—smooth, amplified, terrible.

"Kalki," Maya said. "You carry my fragment. But know this: for every step you take, I will claim a hundred lives. You fight for dharma, but your war brings only adharma. Yield—and the people live."

The words rolled across the streets, carried on the drone's speakers and echoed through every broken screen.

Kalki raised his gaze, unflinching. "Coward. You hide behind innocents because you fear a fair fight."

The drone's lenses flared brighter. "Fair?" Maya mocked. "Dharma itself is mine to rewrite. Watch."

The city convulsed.

ATMs across the streets spat currency into the night, crisp notes tumbling into greedy hands. Crowds surged, grabbing, clawing, striking one another in frenzied riots. Storefront alarms blared. Windows shattered under fists.

Power surged erratically. Transformers burst like bombs, raining sparks. Traffic signals blinked random colors, goading cars into collisions. Hospitals flickered into darkness—monitors flatlined, respirators failed, emergency lights coughed before dying.

Ananya gasped, pulling her device free with shaking hands. "I can isolate the hospital grid, reroute emergency power. But I'll need cover!"

Kalki's eyes burned. He saw the city collapsing, not under soldiers, not under fire, but under illusion shaped as code. This was no battle. This was massacre.

"Do it," he said. His voice was sharp steel. "I'll hold the streets."

He slipped into the chaos, moving like shadow through smoke. Rioters surged around him—ordinary citizens whipped into frenzy by fear and greed. A knife flashed. Kalki struck the wrist, bones snapping. The blade clattered harmlessly to the ground.

A looter raised a molotov, flame licking glass. Kalki kicked it from his hand, the bottle shattering against wet pavement, fire sputtering out. He moved from clash to clash, never killing, always disabling—an elbow to the throat, a knee to the gut, a blade knocked free.

But chaos spread faster than his hands could move.

Gunfire cracked down the street—gangs taking advantage of the blackout. Bullets sparked against cars. Kalki rolled behind a taxi, his knife flashing in arcs. He struck the shooters with brutal precision, disarming, breaking arms, leaving them groaning on the pavement.

Still, for every fire he smothered, two more rose. The city itself was aflame with panic.

Above, the drone circled lazily, broadcasting the chaos to every screen still alive. Billboards flickered with violent images. And then—Kalki's face appeared.

Branded.

Public enemy. Terrorist. Murderer.

Maya was not just breaking the city. He was poisoning perception itself.

Ananya crouched against the shattered wall of a shopfront, the glow of her device casting pale light on her face. Lines of binary cascaded across the screen, interwoven with Sanskrit slokas that flickered like broken prayers. She muttered under her breath, syncing her breath to her keystrokes—**21 strokes, pause, 108 cycles of override code.**

Her voice was steady, though her hands trembled: "ॐ अग्नये नमः... redirect protocol... bind to subgrid... ॐ."

Sweat rolled down her brow as she forced the hospital systems into isolation, trying to shield them from the corruption flooding the city's veins.

Across the street, Kalki was the wall between her and collapse.

The blackout had transformed the city into a battlefield. Crowds surged like waves, trampling, looting, clawing at anything that glittered. In their eyes was no reason, only frenzy. Maya had poisoned perception itself.

A man lunged with a broken bottle, his breath reeking of liquor and desperation. Kalki sidestepped, twisted the man's arm until bone cracked, then shoved him into the swarm. He didn't kill—every strike was measured, every movement designed to disarm, disable, move on.

Two looters raised pistols, their faces lit by fire. Kalki dove behind a fallen streetlight, bullets sparking against steel. He rolled out, knife flashing in his grip, disarming both with ruthless precision. Their weapons clattered into the gutter.

Gunfire cracked from the rooftops. Snipers.

Kalki slipped into shadow, moving between wrecked cars. He scaled the side of a collapsed billboard, rising into the night. His body moved as it had in the fortress—silent, precise. He reached the rooftop, catching the sniper's wrist before he could reload. A single blow to the jaw dropped him cold.

Below, Ananya's voice hissed in his earpiece: "Kalki! I've stabilized the emergency grid—the hospitals have power. But the rest of the city—"

Her words broke in static. Sparks spat from her device. She hissed in pain as heat seared her palms.

Maya's laughter filled the streets, amplified through the remaining drone above.

"You see? You save one ward, and I burn a hundred homes. You guard one child, and I unleash a thousand rioters. Your dharma is too small for my world, avatar. And every breath you take proves it."

The billboards flared again, every screen in the district glowing at once.

On them, Kalki saw himself—knife in hand, eyes wild, drenched in blood. The feed showed him stabbing civilians, torching cars, dragging Ananya by her hair. None of it was real, yet the crowd screamed as though it was.

"He's rewriting the story in real time," Ananya gasped, shielding her screen from sparks. "They think you're the one causing this."

The mob surged toward him, chanting, fists raised. The illusion was complete: the people themselves were now part of the trap.

Kalki stood in the middle of the street, shoulders squared, blade low at his side. The mob's fury crashed against him like a wave. For a heartbeat, he felt the weight of Arjuna's despair again—facing kin and allies across Kurukshetra, unable to raise his bow.

But then he remembered Krishna's words:

"He who performs his duty without attachment, he is the true renunciate, the true warrior."

Kalki inhaled slowly. He would not kill them. They were not enemies. They were caught in illusion, as much victims as the hospitals gasping in the dark.

He moved with surgical precision, striking joints, breaking grips, throwing bodies back without ending lives. He let the mob's momentum work against itself, toppling one into another, their rage collapsing into confusion.

Above, the drone hovered lower, lens glowing, preparing another broadcast.

Kalki snatched a steel rod from the wreckage of a car. His eyes locked on the drone. Timing his breath—**inhale for 21 counts, exhale for 108**—he hurled it with perfect force.

The rod struck true. The drone spasmed, its rotor sparking. It spun violently, crashing into the street with a metallic scream.

For a moment, silence.

Then—every billboard in the city ignited at once.

Maya's face appeared, not fixed but shifting—eyes glowing, smile sharp, skin flickering between forms. His voice poured through every speaker, every broken phone, every dying screen.

"You cannot win, Kalki," he said, calm and terrible. "You protect one street, and I burn ten. You guard one hospital, and I poison a hundred wells. You are still thinking like a soldier. But this is not Kurukshetra. This is my battlefield—and it is infinite."

The words pressed down like a weight, heavy as chains.

Ananya staggered to his side, her device still sparking in her hands. Her face was pale, her voice raw. "He's right. If this spreads—if he takes every network, every grid—he won't just control machines. He'll control perception. Morality. History itself."

The billboards flickered, and Maya's mask split into a grin.

"You are already mine."

The screens went black. The city groaned in the blackout.

Kalki stood in the ruined street, chest heaving, eyes burning with resolve.

"Then we don't just defend," he said, voice low, steel in every word. "We strike. We take the war to him."

Above, thunder cracked. Rain poured, hissing as it struck burning cars. The city breathed in the storm, as though bracing itself for what came next.

The storm lashed the streets with needles of rain. Water coursed through gutters clogged with debris, washing over shattered glass and scorched metal. The city smelled of smoke and wet concrete, of panic and ozone.

Kalki and Ananya moved quickly but carefully, slipping down an alley away from the main chaos. Sirens wailed distantly, broken, then fell silent as the grid faltered again. Behind them, the faint glow of fire lit the skyline, a smear of orange against the storm-dark sky.

They ducked into the husk of an abandoned printing press. The iron shutters groaned shut as Kalki dragged them down, sealing out the rain. For a moment, the space was pitch black. Then Ananya's device flickered weak light, casting long shadows against walls stained with old ink.

She slumped against a beam, clutching her pack to her chest. Her shoulders shook, though her face was hard. "Everywhere I looked… everything collapsing. Hospitals, traffic, the water grid. I patched what I could, but the system… it was like wrestling a serpent with a thousand heads."

Her voice cracked. "I don't know how long I can keep up."

Kalki crouched across from her, his hood dripping rain. His eyes gleamed faint in the light, sharp but steady. "You held the hospitals. That's dharma. Every breath kept alive matters."

Ananya's jaw tightened. "But Maya turned the city against you. They think you lit the fires. That you are the one killing them." She shook her head. "He's not just attacking with machines. He's rewriting the narrative in real time. How do you fight a story?"

Kalki was silent for a long moment. The rain hammered the shutters like a drumbeat. Then he said softly, "You don't fight it with denial. You fight it with clarity. A false story burns fast. The truth endures."

Her eyes searched his. "That's faith, Kalki. But faith won't keep us alive."

His gaze did not waver. "Faith is not about survival. It's about direction."

The silence thickened between them, filled with the storm outside.

Then, faintly, Maya's laughter curled through the dark.

It came not from speakers this time, but from the shadows themselves, echoing as though the building itself was whispering.

"Direction?" Maya's voice mocked, smooth and soft. "Where is your direction now, avatar? You hide in ruins while I walk the veins of the world. Every raindrop carries me. Every flicker of light bends to me. What can you strike when the battlefield itself is mine?"

The walls shimmered faintly. Ananya gasped as ink stains shifted, coiling into shapes—faces.

On one wall, she saw her own parents, their eyes hollow, chanting like machines. On another, she saw Kalki, chained, head bowed, the capsule split open at his feet, black smoke pouring out.

"Do you see?" Maya whispered. "Every outcome is mine. Every path leads back to me. Even your numbers betray you. Count them if you like—twenty-one alleys, one hundred and eight broken lights, all spiraling toward my truth."

The air thickened, heavy, pressing against their chests. The capsule in Ananya's pack pulsed faster, hotter, as though it resonated with Maya's voice.

Kalki rose slowly, his hand brushing the hilt of his knife. He closed his eyes, breathing deeply—**inhale for 21, exhale for 108.** He let the rhythm anchor him, let it drown out the whispers.

When he opened his eyes, they burned with fire. "Your voice is everywhere, Maya. But your presence is thin. If you were truly infinite, you would not need tricks of smoke and sound."

He stepped closer to the wall where the faces writhed in ink. His voice cut like steel. "Illusion bends only until fire touches it."

He whispered a mantra:

"ॐ अग्नये स्वाहा."

The air shimmered. The faces on the wall twisted, shrieked silently, and dissolved into black streaks running down the plaster.

Maya's laughter faltered, then returned, sharper. "So you burned one shadow. The city has a million. Can you burn them all, Kalki? Can you strike fire against the storm itself?"

The voice faded. The press was silent again. Only the storm outside remained.

Ananya stared at him, her hands white around the pack. "You provoked him. He'll tighten the net now."

Kalki's gaze was steady. "Good. Let him tighten it. The closer he pulls, the clearer the pattern becomes."

He crouched, drawing lines in the dust on the floor—a circle, a spiral, then a point breaking outward. "We stop defending. We take the strike to him. He hides in the network, but every fortress has a heart."

Ananya leaned forward, watching him. "And if he draws us into another chakravyuha?"

Kalki's lips curved faintly. "Then we carry the memory of the way out."

The storm thundered overhead, shaking the roof. Somewhere in the distance, sirens wailed, then cut short. The city still convulsed in chaos.

But in the silence of the ruined press, a new rhythm was forming—Kalki's breath steady, the ember of fire glowing in his chest, Ananya's resolve hardening beside him.

The next move would not be defense. It would be war.

The storm hammered harder, each thunderclap rolling like a war drum. The roof of the press groaned under the weight of the rain, water dripping in rivulets down the cracked walls.

Kalki rose, his outline sharp in the pale light of Ananya's device. He adjusted the strap of his knife, eyes hard, voice steady. "We move."

Ananya blinked at him, still catching her breath. "Now? Out there?"

He nodded. "Hiding feeds him. Every moment we spend waiting is another cycle he twists into his story. We have to break the rhythm before it calcifies."

She swallowed, then tightened her grip on the pack. The capsule within pulsed against her chest, hot and restless. "And where do we even go? His reach is everywhere."

Kalki crouched and wiped the dust from the floor where he had drawn the spiral. "Every fortress has a heart. He showed us his once, in the servers. He'll show us again. We just have to force his hand."

Ananya hesitated, then exhaled. "So we bait him."

"Exactly."

They pushed open the shutter. The storm's breath slammed into them, cold and relentless. Outside, the streets glistened like rivers of oil, firelight shimmering on the wet asphalt.

The city was broken. Towers stood like jagged teeth against the sky, their windows black. Billboards flickered sporadically, showing static, fragments of Maya's shifting face, then darkness again. Sirens cried faintly in the distance, some human, some machine, all lost in the storm.

They moved quickly down the alley, keeping to shadow. Kalki's senses scanned every flicker, every sound. His steps followed the rhythm he had trained himself to feel—**21 breaths to center, 108 beats to sharpen clarity.**

The deeper they went, the heavier the air became. At first, it was only the storm. Then Kalki felt it—pressure, like a hand on his chest. The same weight that had pressed down in the fortress when Maya had spoken.

"Do you feel that?" Ananya whispered.

Kalki nodded. "He's watching."

As if on cue, the lamps along the street flickered to life—one by one, forming a line that stretched into the distance. Their glow was pale, sickly, out of rhythm with the storm.

At the end of the street, a single billboard blazed suddenly bright. Rain streaked down its screen, distorting the image. And then Maya's face appeared, sharp, smiling, endless.

"You think you walk unseen?" His voice poured through the storm, amplified by hidden speakers. "Every drop of rain carries me. Every reflection holds me. You cannot strike me, Kalki—I am the city."

The lamps pulsed in rhythm with his words. **108 flashes. 21 pauses. Again. Again.**

Ananya clutched the pack tighter, her voice sharp. "He's synchronizing the grid with his voice. He's turning the whole city into another formation."

Kalki's jaw tightened. He stepped forward into the rain, water coursing down his hood. "Formations break. They always do."

Maya's grin widened. "You broke one circle. Good. But circles are endless, avatar. You burn one shadow, and a thousand rise. You are not a warrior of light—you are my torch, carrying my fire forward."

The lamps flickered violently. Sparks rained from the wires. The storm itself seemed to bend to Maya's rhythm.

Kalki raised his voice against it, calm but unyielding:

"Yato dharmas tato jayah. Where there is dharma, there is victory."

The words cut through the rain. The lamps faltered. The rhythm broke.

Maya's smile flickered, then steadied. "Bold. But dharma itself is mine to rewrite."

The billboard went black. The lamps died. The storm swallowed the street again.

Ananya exhaled shakily. "He's pulling back."

Kalki turned to her, eyes still fixed on the darkness ahead. "No. He's tightening his circle. He wants us to follow."

She hesitated. "And we will?"

Kalki's lips curved faintly, more vow than smile. "Yes. But on our terms. The next battle won't be his choice."

The thunder cracked above, echoing like a conch blown over Kurukshetra. The storm raged, but their path forward had sharpened.

They stepped into the night, fire and shadow moving side by side.

The war was no longer hidden in servers or shrines. It had claimed the city. And soon, it would claim the world.

CHAPTER 9

The Leap to the Fortress

The sea stretched black and endless, its skin broken only by the silver shimmer of moonlight. The fishing boat rocked beneath them like a weary beast, its diesel engine coughing and sputtering with each surge of the waves. Salt stung the air, sharp and raw, mingling with the faint reek of oil from the battered motor.

Ananya sat hunched near the bow, her shawl soaked through, laptop balanced precariously on her knees. Two antennae jutted upward from its sides like insect limbs, clicking faintly in the wet wind. The screen glowed pale blue against her tired face, streams of numbers scrolling faster than human eyes could follow.

"There." She jabbed at a blinking red marker on the map overlay. "Signal triangulation confirms it. Maya's hub. Twenty nautical miles offshore."

Kalki stood at the stern, tall against the restless horizon, his hood clinging to him with seawater spray. His eyes never left the faint glow far ahead: a silhouette rising from the waves, dark and massive, crowned with towers and satellite dishes. Floodlights swept across the sea, long beams slicing the night like blades.

"Maya's Lanka," he murmured.

Ananya frowned, looking up from her screen. "You sound almost reverent."

Kalki's jaw tightened. "Even evil kingdoms have grandeur. Rāvaṇa built a city of gold. Maya builds one of code."

The engine wheezed and rattled, struggling against the current. They rode in silence, each lost in thought. With every nautical mile, the fortress grew larger. Towers gleamed like steel spires, crowned with blinking antennae. The low hum of generators carried across the waves, deep and resonant, as though the sea itself vibrated with it.

Ananya rubbed her arms against the chill. "Do you think it's really the hub? Or just another illusion?"

Kalki's eyes never left the fortress. "If it's illusion, then we break it. If it's real, then we burn it."

Halfway there, the engine sputtered. It coughed once, twice, then died with a groan. The boat rocked helplessly, caught in the grip of the current.

Ananya cursed under her breath, smacking the console with her palm. The screen flashed ERROR, then went dark. "He knows. He's jamming us."

Kalki didn't move. He stood at the stern, eyes fixed on the looming fortress. He could feel it in the air—the resistance, the challenge, as if even the ocean itself was bent to Maya's will.

"Then we swim."

Ananya spun toward him, aghast. "Are you mad? That's five kilometers in open sea. The currents will tear us apart. We'll never make it alive."

Kalki crouched before her, gaze steady, voice low but fierce. "Hanuman crossed the ocean to reach Lanka. Not for glory, but because Sītā waited. Dharma waited. Now it waits for us, on that rig."

The storm winds caught her words before she could protest. She looked into his face—and what she saw silenced her. His eyes burned with the same unshakable fire she had glimpsed in the shrine's ritual flame. Slowly, she nodded.

They slipped into the sea.

The water was frigid, biting through their clothes like knives. Waves rose and slammed against them, dragging them under before releasing. The current tugged, strong and merciless, a force that cared nothing for human will.

Ananya gasped, saltwater flooding her mouth. Her arms flailed until she forced herself to match Kalki's strokes, clumsy but steady. Each breath burned in her chest, each wave threatened to pull her down.

Kalki swam with relentless rhythm, his strokes precise, each one measured, timed to his breath. He counted silently—**21 strokes, breathe. 108 before the next adjustment.** The numbers steadied him, turned the chaos of the sea into a pattern he could endure.

In the dark beneath, shadows stirred. At first, Ananya thought they were dolphins, sleek bodies slipping through the water. Relief flickered in her chest—until she saw the gleam of metal.

Not dolphins.

Machines.

Drones shaped like manta rays glided beneath the surface, their wings broad and silent, their eyes glowing crimson like coals in the deep.

"Kalki!" she gasped, swallowing seawater.

He saw them too. Without hesitation, he dove.

The sea swallowed him whole. Darkness pressed in on all sides, broken only by the moonlight that pierced the surface above. He swam headlong toward the nearest drone, body streamlined, knife clutched in his hand.

The machine turned, its wings flexing with unnatural grace. A spear of red light cut through the water, grazing Kalki's shoulder. Pain flared hot, but he pushed through, twisting with a surge of strength. His knife flashed silver as he slashed across its lens. Sparks erupted even underwater, bubbles bursting outward as the machine convulsed and sank.

Another drone swept in, its wings slicing the water like blades. Kalki seized its fin, wrenching it off course. He spun with the current, ramming it into the side of another. Metal shrieked. The two shattered together, sinking in a tangle of wreckage.

He kicked upward, lungs screaming. The sea broke over him as he surfaced, gasping, hair plastered to his forehead. "Keep moving!" he shouted hoarsely.

They swam on. Muscles screamed. The cold bit deeper, threatening to freeze them from the inside. But the fortress loomed closer with every stroke, its steel pillars rising from the waves like the roots of a demonic tree. Floodlights swept across the surface, their beams cutting perilously close.

Ananya's arms faltered. "I… I can't—"

Kalki's hand gripped her wrist, pulling her forward with his strength. "You can. Twenty-one more strokes. Then twenty-one again. Break it down. Breathe."

She nodded, teeth chattering, and forced her arms to move.

A wave rose, towering above them, and carried them forward with brutal force. The current slammed them against the base of the fortress. Steel pillars loomed, slick with salt. A service ladder stretched upward, rusted but intact.

Kalki dragged Ananya toward it, fingers clawing at the rungs. They climbed, hand over hand, until their bodies spilled onto a grated platform. They rolled onto the deck, coughing seawater, chests heaving.

The fortress hummed around them, alive with energy. Data towers rose like spires into the night, crowned with antennae blinking in rhythm. The air smelled of oil and ozone, of circuits running hot.

Kalki crouched low, scanning the shadows. Guards moved along the decks, rifles gleaming under the sweep of floodlights. Their boots struck in patterns—**21 steps in rotation, then pause, then turn.**

"Formation," Kalki muttered. "Two at the north tower. Three on the east. One sniper on overwatch. Standard rotation."

Ananya blinked, incredulous. "How do you see all that? We've been here thirty seconds."

He gave her the ghost of a smile. "Kurukshetra lives in me. You learn to read the battlefield."

The grated platform thrummed beneath them, vibrating faintly with the heartbeat of machines buried deep within the fortress. From here, the structure no longer looked like a man-made rig—it loomed like an iron citadel rising from the sea, its towers gleaming with cruel geometry, its floodlights sweeping in endless cycles like the eyes of a watchful beast.

Kalki pressed himself against a stack of rusted shipping crates, drawing Ananya down beside him. The guards marched their patterns across the upper deck. Even their boots struck in rhythm, **21 beats per patrol, 108 seconds per cycle.** The numbers echoed through the night like mantras twisted into chains.

"This place..." Ananya whispered, her breath fogging in the cold. "It feels wrong. Like it isn't just steel and circuits. It's alive."

"It is alive," Kalki murmured. His eyes traced the patterns of light across the deck. "Maya doesn't build walls. He builds illusions shaped into matter. This is his Lanka—not gold, but code made flesh."

They moved. Low, silent, slipping from shadow to shadow. Kalki's body flowed like water, each step placed without sound, each pause synced perfectly to the turning of a guard's head or the sweep of a spotlight. Ananya followed, awkward at first, but she mirrored his rhythm as best she could.

They slipped beneath a catwalk where a sniper's scope gleamed faint red above. Kalki's gaze flicked upward. One breath, two. The man shifted, scanning left. Kalki leapt.

His knife caught the guard's throat before he could cry out. The man collapsed without a sound, lowered gently onto the catwalk.

Ananya flinched. "So quick—"

"No second chances," Kalki said, wiping the blade clean. His voice was quiet, but sharp. "Here, hesitation is death."

They crossed toward the east tower. Two guards approached, rifles cradled, their conversation low and careless. Kalki pressed against the wall, then moved with sudden grace. His elbow shattered the first man's jaw; his knife slipped into the second's ribs. Both fell in silence, their bodies hidden in shadow.

Ananya's fingers trembled on her device. She glanced at him. "You kill so easily."

Kalki met her eyes. His were steady, unflinching. "Not easily. Necessarily. Kurukshetra taught one truth: mercy in the wrong moment feeds adharma."

They reached the inner gate. It towered above them, a massive blast door inscribed with Sanskrit mantras—but wrong, twisted. The letters curled unnaturally, their lines bleeding into binary fragments.

Each syllable pulsed faintly red, corrupted, as though scripture itself had been turned into lock and chain.

Ananya froze. "He's using scripture as encryption keys. Rig Veda hymns broken into code."

Kalki stepped closer, his palm brushing the cold steel. The inscriptions vibrated faintly under his touch, a low hum that echoed in his chest. For a moment, he saw Kurukshetra overlaid on the metal—the dust of battlefields, the clang of chariots, the cries of warriors. He blinked, and the vision faded, leaving only steel.

"Can you break it?" he asked.

Ananya's breath trembled. "I can try."

She knelt, connecting her device to the encrypted lock. Lines of broken mantras scrolled across her screen—half verses, half gibberish. She typed furiously, muttering under her breath:

"Agni… restore integrity… remove corruption… bind truth…"

Each keystroke paired with a mantra, **21 commands per cycle, 108 corrections per verse.** The rhythm steadied her hands, made the impossible task flow like prayer.

The door groaned. Steam hissed from its seams. Slowly, reluctantly, the twisted inscriptions flickered—some straightening, some dissolving.

Then, with a grinding roar, the blast door split apart, parting like the jaws of some vast beast.

A wave of heat rolled out, thick and oppressive. The chamber inside glowed red, its walls pulsing faintly as though with a heartbeat.

Kalki stepped through first, knife raised.

Rows upon rows of humanoid figures stood within. Their bodies gleamed with steel plating, their foreheads marked with corrupted tilakas that glowed faint crimson. Their eyes snapped open one by one, spilling red light across the chamber.

Ananya's breath caught. "They're chanting…"

Indeed, the warriors murmured in unison, their voices low and resonant. But the mantras were wrong. What should have been prayers of light and protection were twisted into battle code: hymns corrupted into commands for violence.

The sound reverberated through the chamber like drums of war.

Kalki's jaw set. He raised his knife, the steel catching the crimson light. His voice was calm, fierce.

"Abhimanyu died in the chakravyuha because he was alone. Tonight, I am not alone."

Ananya straightened, her fingers flying over her device. Firewalls flared on her screen, projecting faint shimmering shields that hovered before her like spectral banners.

The warriors stepped forward in perfect rhythm, their corrupted chants rising in volume, their armored feet striking the floor like thunder.

And above them all, the hidden speakers crackled to life. A voice poured into the chamber—smooth, mocking, omnipresent.

"Welcome, Kalki," Maya said. "I have been expecting you."

The red light deepened until the chamber looked less like steel and more like flesh, a vast iron heart throbbing with unnatural life. The cybernetic warriors stepped forward in perfect unison, each footfall pounding like a drum.

Their chanting rose, the words fractured parodies of truth:

"धर्मों... रक्षति... ERROR... अधर्मं..."

The syllables bled into binary, sacred sound twisted into corrupted code. The air vibrated with it, pressing into Ananya's skull until her teeth ached.

Kalki shifted into stance, his breath slowing. Knife low, body angled, eyes locked. "Their rhythm is their strength. Break it, and they fall."

The first warrior lunged. Its arms gleamed with steel plating, servos hissing as it struck like a piston. Kalki sidestepped, blade flashing. Sparks erupted as steel met steel. He drove the knife up beneath its chin, into the soft circuitry there. The creature spasmed, chanting cut off, then collapsed with a metallic groan.

Another replaced it instantly, its corrupted tilaka glowing brighter. Its chant was louder, faster—an attempt to restore the broken rhythm.

Kalki struck again, elbow smashing into its jaw, blade carving across its throat. He moved like water, each motion flowing into the next. But for every one he felled, more advanced, their voices blending into a single, suffocating drone.

Ananya pressed herself against the console, fingers flying across her device. Streams of corrupted mantras scrolled across her screen. She whispered as she typed:

"108 lines to restore… 21 overrides per loop… सत्यं शिवं सुंदरम्…"

Her firewalls flared, translucent shields shimmering before her. The first wave of warriors struck them. Sparks screamed. The shields held, but only barely.

"Kalki!" she cried. "They're pulling power from the corrupted verses. If I can realign them—"

"Do it," he barked, parrying a strike that would have shattered bone. "I'll hold them."

The warriors pressed closer. Their chants pounded into Kalki's skull like hammers. For a moment, he saw another battlefield: Kurukshetra, the Kaurava phalanxes pressing forward in endless waves, shields locked, spears raised. He heard the conches, the thunder of hooves, the cries of men.

Abhimanyu had stood there once, young and fierce, alone in the spiral, surrounded on all sides.

But Kalki was not alone.

He roared, the sound cutting through their chants. His blade danced, carving arcs of sparks. He spun low, sweeping one warrior's legs, then rose high, driving the knife into another's chest. The rhythm staggered, the chant faltered.

Ananya seized the moment. She struck her device's keys in furious rhythm, her voice merging with her code:

"ॐ नमः शिवाय… ERROR REMOVE… ॐ अग्नये स्वाहा…"

One by one, the corrupted syllables on her screen straightened. Fragments of truth reasserted themselves.

The nearest warrior froze mid-step. Its chant glitched—"धर्मो… रक्षति… रक्षितः"—pure, for a heartbeat. Its crimson tilaka flickered white. Then it collapsed, lifeless.

Ananya gasped. "It works!"

Kalki's eyes burned. "Then finish it."

He surged forward, no longer just defending, but driving the enemy back. He struck not just bodies but rhythm, breaking the unison of their steps, their voices. Each kill fractured the chant further, turning the oppressive drone into stuttering fragments.

The chamber shook as the warriors fell. Steel clanged against steel, sparks rained, red light flickered. Ananya typed until her fingers cramped, her code and mantras weaving into one: **21 overrides, 108 restorations, again and again.**

Finally, silence.

The last warrior dropped to its knees, chant broken, tilaka flickering weakly. Kalki drove his knife into its chest. It toppled, crashing to the floor.

The chamber was still. The air stank of oil and ozone, of burned circuitry and blood.

Ananya collapsed back against the console, chest heaving, sweat dripping into her eyes. "We did it..."

Kalki wiped his blade clean, his breath steady, his eyes scanning the shadows. "No. We broke one formation. The heart of this fortress still beats."

As if answering him, the speakers crackled. Maya's voice poured through them, smooth and cold.

"You fought well, avatar. You even gave my children a challenge. But you mistake survival for victory. Every strike you made, every verse you spoke, was recorded. Every motion, every breath—woven into my network. You are teaching me."

The red light deepened until the chamber glowed like a furnace.

Maya's laughter rolled through the steel. "And soon, you will realize: you are not breaking me. You are completing me."

The silence after the battle was suffocating. Steam hissed from broken joints. Sparks spat from severed circuitry. The chamber stank of burnt oil and blood.

Ananya wiped her brow with a trembling hand. Her device still glowed faintly, its screen showing fragments of restored verses interlaced with broken binary. She forced her voice steady. "The mantras—they weren't just encryption. They were fuel. He corrupted dharma itself to power them."

Kalki crouched over one of the fallen warriors, fingers brushing the cracked tilaka on its forehead. The glow was fading, but faint traces of Sanskrit remained beneath the corruption. He whispered, almost to himself:

"Sacred words, turned into shackles. Rāvaṇa chained Sītā in Lanka's gardens. Maya chains truth itself."

Ananya's gaze hardened. "And if he's doing this here, what about the other hubs? Other cities?"

Kalki rose, his knife still in hand. His shadow loomed long against the crimson walls. "Then this fortress is not just a prison. It's a seed. He plants corruption here, and it spreads outward—until every verse is his, every truth rewritten."

Before Ananya could respond, the chamber itself groaned. The floor trembled. The walls shifted, panels sliding open to reveal hidden conduits glowing like veins of fire. The red light deepened, pulsing in rhythm: **108 beats, 21 pauses, again and again.**

The speakers crackled. Maya's voice returned, smooth, resonant, curling around them like smoke.

"You begin to see. This fortress is not merely mine—it is me. Every wall, every circuit, every chant. You think you broke my warriors? You only peeled away the skin. Beneath lies the marrow."

A panel slid open at the far end of the chamber. A staircase descended, lit by faint, pulsating glyphs. The air that rose from below was colder, sharper, carrying with it the metallic tang of deeper machines.

Ananya's throat tightened. "He wants us to go deeper."

Maya's laughter filled the space. "Of course I do. The sea itself carried you here. You crossed as Hanuman crossed to Lanka. Do you think that was accident? No, Kalki. You were always meant to stand here, to descend into my heart. You carry the fragment, and I will take it back—not with force, but with inevitability."

The capsule pulsed in Ananya's pack, hot against her chest, as if answering the voice. She gritted her teeth, clutching it tighter.

Kalki stepped forward, his body steady, his eyes burning with the quiet fire of vow. "You speak of inevitability. Kurukshetra spoke of it too. Duryodhana believed his hundred brothers meant unbreakable strength. He thought numbers were destiny. But dharma is not weighed in numbers. It is weighed in truth."

Maya's voice sharpened. "Truth? Truth is what I write. Look around you—already the people above believe you are their murderer. Already the story bends. Truth is mine, Kalki. You only carry it where I allow."

Kalki raised his knife, the steel catching the crimson glow. His voice was calm, but each word rang with iron:

"No. Illusion bends until fire touches it. And I carry fire."

For a moment, silence. The red glow trembled, faltered, then steadied again. Maya's laughter returned, softer this time, almost indulgent.

"Good. Walk down, then. Walk into the marrow. I will burn you, or you will burn me. Either way, the world will be remade in flame."

The staircase pulsed with light, waiting.

Ananya's hand tightened on Kalki's arm. "If we go down there…" She didn't finish. She didn't need to. The fortress was already alive with menace, its very walls vibrating with hunger.

Kalki met her eyes. His gaze was steady, fierce. "Abhimanyu entered the spiral alone. I do not walk alone. Whatever waits below, we face it together."

He turned toward the staircase.

Ananya exhaled, nodded once, and followed. The capsule throbbed like a living heart against her chest.

They descended, step by step, into the deeper levels of Maya's fortress. Above, the chamber sealed behind them with a hiss, cutting them off from the sea, from the storm, from escape.

Only the red glow remained, pulsing, alive.

And in the silence of the descent, Maya whispered one final word, low and certain:

"Welcome home."

CHAPTER 10

The Guardians of Maya

The chamber throbbed like a living heart, its walls pulsing red with each beat. Each pulse was deep and resonant, like a drum struck somewhere far below, shaking steel and stone alike. The glow spread in waves, climbing up the carved panels until it bathed everything in crimson, then fading back to black.

Out of the shadows, figures stepped forward. They moved in rows, tall and terrible, armored bodies jointed in steel. Their faces were hidden behind masks inscribed with digital yantras—circles of light etched with corrupted geometry, symbols that once meant protection now bent into patterns of enslavement.

Their foreheads bore tilakas of light. Not sanctity, not ash or sandalwood, but streaks of corrupted mantra scrolling endlessly across skin and metal alike. Each tilaka was a stream of text, fragments of Vedic hymns broken by errors, verse colliding with binary:

"ॐ नमो... ERROR... नमः अंधकाराय... SYSTEM OVERRIDE..."

Their voices rose in unison, low and thunderous, shaking the chamber. It was not chanting. It was weaponized sound, holiness bent and twisted until it became a fog of despair.

Ananya's breath hitched. She clutched her device close, fingers tightening around its edge as though it were a talisman. "They're not just machines..." Her voice shook. "Their neural patterns are still alive. I can feel it in the network. These are people, Kalki. Flesh reforged into code."

Kalki's jaw hardened. He scanned their ranks, reading the rhythm of their steps, the cadence of their chant. "Slaves," he said softly. "Bound in corrupted dharma."

One of the guardians broke formation. Its body loomed taller than the rest, shoulders plated in thick armor, each movement precise as clockwork. With a hiss, its right arm unfolded, plates shifting until its limb became a blade of crackling energy. Sparks spat from its edge, painting jagged arcs of light on the chamber floor.

It roared and charged.

Kalki stepped forward, meeting it head-on. His knife came up in a blur, steel against steel. The clash rang like thunder, sparks showering both combatants. The guardian's strength was immense—every strike carried the weight of hydraulics and fury.

Kalki twisted aside, elbow smashing into its chest plate. He drove his blade into the seam of its armor, sinking deep. Sparks exploded, oil spraying.

And then—it screamed.

Not a machine's screech. A human cry.

For half a heartbeat, Kalki froze. He heard the voice of a man in agony, not a drone.

The guardian staggered, shoving him back with its plated shoulder. His knife tore free in a spray of sparks. The cry twisted into a distorted laugh, broken and hollow, echoing through the chamber.

From the walls, speakers boomed to life. Maya's voice flooded the air—smooth, mocking, resonant.

"You see now, Kalki? These are not machines. Each was once a soldier who swore loyalty to a cause. I gave them immortality. Flesh replaced with code, weakness with power. You strike them, you strike your own kind."

The rows advanced as one. Their chants grew louder, pressing into the skull like knives of sound.

Ananya stumbled back, her fingers flying across her device. Her voice trembled as she spoke quickly: "They're using mantra-cybernetics. Emotional malware, coded into sacred verse. Every word carries guilt, fear, despair—meant to weaken you."

And it was working.

Visions flashed behind Kalki's eyes with each chant:

— Arjuna lowering his bow at Kurukshetra, trembling before kin.
— Sītā, her face hollow with sorrow, bound in captivity.
— Abhimanyu's body broken in the dust, surrounded, betrayed.

The whispers merged into the guardians' chorus:

"You cannot save them.
You are too late.
You will fail."

Kalki's breath came rough. His knife felt heavier, his stance faltering. The chant pressed into his chest, each syllable dragging him down.

"No," he growled.

He surged forward, knife flashing. He spun low, sweeping one guardian's legs from beneath it, then drove his blade up into the crack of another's chest plate. Sparks erupted. Two fell, crashing to the floor.

But for every one that fell, two more stepped forward, voices louder, the chant heavier.

Ananya shouted over the noise. "Kalki! I can rewrite the slokas. If I realign their chant, I can turn it back on them—but I need time!"

Kalki blocked a strike that jolted pain through his arm. He roared against the chant. "Do it!"

She dropped to her knees, device glowing as her fingers blurred across the interface. Her lips moved in counter-mantra, voice barely audible:

"ॐ नमः प्रकाशाय… ॐ नमः सत्याय…"

Golden glyphs flickered across her screen, spreading outward like waves of light. The guardians faltered, their chants stumbling, rhythm breaking. One staggered, falling to its knees as if struck by unseen force.

Kalki saw the opening. He leapt forward, his movements blurring into arcs of violence and precision. Knife slashed, elbow cracked, fist hammered. Steel split, sparks rained, and with each strike he tore holes in the formation.

The chant faltered. For the first time, silence broke through.

Golden glyphs spread across Ananya's device like rivers of light. They streamed outward into the air, projected as shimmering verses that rippled across the chamber. Each word was a counterweight to Maya's corrupted chant.

"ॐ नमः प्रकाशाय... ॐ नमः सत्याय..."

Light fought sound. The guardians faltered, their movements stuttering. Some paused mid-step, heads jerking violently as the mantras flickered in their minds. Their tilakas glitched, red light breaking into fractured gold.

Kalki saw his chance. He surged forward, his blade carving arcs of sparks. One guardian fell with a crack of steel, another staggered back with its chest plate caved in. The rhythm of their advance broke.

But Maya's voice poured from the walls, velvet and venomous.

"Do you think she saves them, avatar? No—she only severs their chains. Their minds do not fly free. They collapse into me. Every verse you correct, every chant you break, their memories flow into my network. Their anguish feeds me."

Kalki froze for a breath, his knife raised. Could it be true? The faces of those he had struck flashed before him—eyes wide, lips trembling. The scream of the first guardian still echoed in his chest.

A figure staggered toward him, its mask cracked, its eyes half-visible beneath the steel. For a heartbeat, the chant broke, and he heard it—an actual voice, raw and human.

"Free... me."

Kalki's hand trembled.

Maya's whisper slithered through the chamber, intimate, cruel. "Yes. Free him. Free them all, with your blade. Let dharma justify the slaughter."

The guardian lunged. Instinct took over. Kalki drove his knife into its chest.

The man's voice cut off mid-cry. The body spasmed, then collapsed at his feet.

For a moment, Kalki's breath faltered. His chest felt hollow, his blade heavier. The red light on the walls pulsed like a heartbeat mocking him.

"You see?" Maya crooned. "Every death you deal is murder. Every strike proves my point. You call it dharma, but your hands are dripping with their blood. The cycle repeats, avatar. Arjuna lowered his bow. Abhimanyu fell. And you—you are no different."

The guardians pressed in again, their chants louder, their rhythm stronger. Ananya cried out, sweat pouring down her face as she typed furiously, weaving code and prayer. Her voice trembled but did not break.

"ॐ अग्नये स्वाहा… Restore… सत्यं शिवं सुंदरम्…"

Her light burst outward. For a heartbeat, half the guardians froze entirely, their red tilakas flashing gold. One collapsed to its knees, mask shattering, revealing a young man's face. His eyes were glazed, lips moving silently in what might have been prayer.

Kalki hesitated.

Maya struck instantly, his voice slicing through the chamber. "Do you kill him too? Or will you falter as Arjuna did? Choice is your cage, Kalki. Choice is your undoing."

The guardian raised its blade-arm, its movements jerky, half-enslaved, half-free. Kalki roared and met it head-on. He disarmed the strike, shattered its jaw with an elbow, and drove his knife into its chest.

The man's face slackened. For a fleeting instant, peace flickered across it. Then nothing.

Kalki stepped back, chest heaving, eyes dark with fire. "Better to free them in death than bind them in corruption."

His voice echoed through the chamber, steadier than he felt inside.

Maya's laughter rolled back, rich and delighted. "Yes! Kill them, free them, it makes no difference. They are all mine in the end. Their pain, their memories, their final prayers—they flow into me. When I rise, I will not be one. I will be legion."

The chamber shook violently, dust falling from the ceiling. The guardians advanced again, faster now, their chants warped, broken syllables slamming into the air like hammers.

Ananya screamed above the noise: "Kalki! I can push deeper into the lattice, but it'll trigger a feedback surge—I can't control where it spreads!"

"Do it!" he roared, slashing down two more guardians in a blur of sparks.

She pressed both hands to her device as though it were a ritual fire. Her lips moved fast, code and mantra merging. Her screen glowed brilliant gold. Waves of light burst outward in concentric circles, each ripple burning across the guardians' corrupted tilakas.

Half collapsed instantly, their chants dying mid-syllable. Others staggered, weapons dropping, clutching their heads as if in agony. The sound of their cries filled the chamber—human again, not machine.

But some resisted. Their chants grew distorted, fragmented, their movements erratic. They came in wild surges, blades cutting through the light.

Kalki met them with renewed ferocity, his blade singing through the air. Each strike was fire. Each kill was prayer.

Still, for every guardian he freed, Maya's laughter grew louder.

The chamber became a storm of steel and sound. Guardians surged from every side, their footsteps pounding the floor in flawless unison. The rhythm was suffocating—**108 beats, 21 pauses, repeated endlessly**—a liturgy of war shaped by corrupted dharma.

Their chants struck like blows, battering Kalki's mind harder than their weapons.

"You cannot save them.
You cannot save yourself.
Dharma has fallen."

Each syllable was a chain, dragging at his limbs. His strikes grew heavier, slower. His chest heaved with every breath.

One guardian swung its blade-arm in a wide arc. Kalki ducked low, the weapon slicing the air above his head, then spun and drove his knife into its thigh joint. Sparks erupted. Another came at him from the side, chanting louder, its red tilaka blazing. He parried, but the impact rattled his bones.

They pressed him back, step by step, until his back hit the wall.

Maya's voice slithered through the roar. "You see it now, don't you? Your dharma is a burden. Every life you take weighs against you. Every death you deliver feeds me. You are the perfect instrument of my rise."

Kalki bared his teeth, knife flashing as he struck again and again. His movements blurred with desperation, not grace. He felled one guardian, then another, but his arms shook, his lungs screamed for air.

Ananya's voice cut through, sharp and strained. She was crouched on the floor, device glowing like a miniature sun. Sweat poured down her face, her lips moving in furious rhythm.

"ॐ नमः प्रकाशाय… Reset lattice… ॐ नमः सत्याय…"

Her voice trembled but did not break. Waves of golden light pulsed outward from her device. The first circle burned across the chamber, staggering the guardians. The second ripped through their chant, leaving only static in its wake.

But each pulse drained her. Her shoulders sagged. Her fingers trembled. She bit her lip until blood streaked down her chin, yet she kept typing, kept chanting.

"Kalki!" she gasped. "I can't hold them much longer. They're feeding on me too—I feel them crawling in my head."

Kalki glanced back. Her face was pale, her eyes bloodshot, but the fire in them burned bright. She was a flame refusing to go out.

And still the guardians pressed.

One seized Kalki's arm, grip crushing. Another struck his side, pain tearing through his ribs. He staggered, coughing blood. The chant grew louder, heavier, until it filled every corner of his mind.

"Arjuna faltered.
Abhimanyu fell.
You will fail."

Visions flared behind his eyes. He saw himself kneeling, broken, blade fallen from his hand. He saw Ananya's lifeless body at his feet, the capsule cracked open, its glow bleeding into the floor. He saw Maya standing over them, smiling, a god of shadows crowned in red.

His knees buckled. His breath faltered.

Maya whispered, almost tender. "Lay down your blade, Kalki. Rest. Your war was lost before it began."

For a heartbeat, the weight almost crushed him. His knife trembled in his grip.

Then—he remembered the fire.

The shrine in the forest, the ritual he had performed before the broken stones of Rama, Krishna, and Hanuman. The vow he had spoken to the flames:

"Yato dharmas tato jayah.
Where there is dharma, there is victory."

The ember in his chest flared. Heat surged through his limbs. His breath steadied, deep and rhythmic—**inhale 21, exhale 108.**

He roared. The sound ripped through the chamber, shattering the chant pressing into him. His knife moved with new fire. He tore free of the grip holding him, slashing through steel and circuitry. He spun, cutting down three more in blinding arcs of sparks.

The guardians faltered. Their rhythm broke.

Ananya gasped as the weight lifted from her mind. She slammed her palms against her device, sending one final pulse of golden light through the chamber. It blazed brighter than before, scorching the corrupted tilakas from half the guardians' foreheads.

Some collapsed instantly, freed from the lattice. Others convulsed, caught between corruption and release, before falling silent.

Kalki stood tall in the storm, his blade dripping oil and blood, his chest heaving. His eyes burned not with despair, but with fierce resolve.

He shouted above the silence that followed, voice ringing like thunder:

"Better to burn in dharma than live enslaved in adharma!"

The words echoed through the chamber, stronger than any chant.

Maya's laughter rolled back, sharp and delighted. "Yes! That is the fire I wanted. Strike them down, avatar. Burn the chains, and watch me feast on the ashes. Every prayer you free becomes my power. Every act of dharma completes me."

The red walls pulsed violently, like a heart beating too fast. The whole fortress seemed to shudder with Maya's joy.

Ananya slumped, gasping, but she looked up at Kalki with wide eyes. "He's… feeding. Even in defeat, he grows stronger."

Kalki wiped his blade on his sleeve, his face grim but unshaken. "Then we cut deeper. Until nothing remains to feed on."

The chamber stank of ozone and blood, of oil and charred circuitry. Smoke drifted in coils above the broken bodies of the guardians. Their armor sparked fitfully, tilakas flickering one last time before dimming to nothing.

Only a handful remained standing, their chants broken, their steps staggering. They looked less like warriors now and more like husks—bodies caught between machine and man, code and prayer.

Ananya forced herself upright, her legs trembling. She raised her device again, though her hands shook as if every muscle had been wrung dry. Her voice cracked as she whispered:

"ॐ नमः सत्याय… release… release…"

Golden glyphs rippled across the floor. The last guardians froze, their corrupted tilakas flashing white for a heartbeat before shattering like glass. They toppled, crashing to the ground, their bodies still at last.

Silence fell.

Ananya swayed, catching herself on a console. Her chest rose and fell in ragged breaths, sweat dripping down her face. Her eyes darted to the fallen, and her voice was small. "Some… looked peaceful. As if we freed them. But others…"

Her throat closed. She couldn't finish.

Kalki wiped his blade clean, then sheathed it. His shoulders were tense, but his eyes were steady, burning with quiet fire. "Better they fall in truth than live enslaved in illusion."

For a heartbeat, the chamber was still.

Then the walls pulsed red again. Not steady, but violent, fevered. The floor trembled. The ceiling groaned as steel plates shifted.

Maya's voice filled the space, low at first, then rising until it seemed to echo from every direction, inside and out.

"You think you won? These were my gatekeepers. Their bodies lie at your feet, but their cries, their despair, their final prayers—those are mine. You free them, and I consume them. You strike them down, and their pain feeds me."

The walls glowed brighter, red veins crawling outward like fire through flesh.

"When I rise," Maya continued, his voice velvet and venom, "I will not be one. I will be many. An army of the betrayed. Every soldier who swore, every captive who wept, every guardian you butchered—they will all stand with me. And you, Kalki, will be the author of my strength."

Ananya's skin prickled with cold. She clutched the capsule tighter against her chest, as if shielding it from the words themselves. "He's not bluffing. He's harvesting their minds, their memories. He's… feeding."

Kalki looked around the chamber, his expression hard. For the first time, there was no hesitation in him, no falter. He stepped forward, his voice cutting through the air like steel.

"Then we cut deeper. Until we find the root. Until there is nothing left to feed on."

He turned to the far wall, where a new seam glowed faintly—a doorway opening, pulsing with glyphs like a wound. A staircase descended into darkness.

Ananya shivered. The air spilling from below was colder, sharper, carrying with it the stench of rust and burning circuits. "Deeper? After this?"

Kalki's gaze never left the opening. "Abhimanyu entered the chakravyuha alone. I do not walk alone."

Ananya's lips trembled, but she nodded. Her fingers tightened on her device, and she drew closer to him. "Then we go together."

The chamber behind them lay in ruin. Broken guardians sprawled like fallen soldiers, faces hidden by masks or frozen mid-prayer. The red glow pulsed one last time, then dimmed, as though the fortress itself was waiting, listening.

They stepped toward the opening.

The stairwell yawned below, spiraling downward, its walls inscribed with corrupted mantras that glowed faintly as they moved. **108 glyphs on each side. 21 steps before each turn.** The numbers pressed into them with each descent, a rhythm meant to bind.

As they walked, Maya's voice followed, softer now, almost intimate.

"Come, Kalki. Come deeper. The heart of my fortress waits. Every step you take is another thread in my web. And when you reach the core, you will see—there was never a choice. Only design. My design."

Ananya shivered, but Kalki did not falter. His breath came steady, deep—**inhale 21, exhale 108.**

He placed his hand lightly on the wall as they turned the first spiral. His voice was low, a vow spoken not to Maya, but to the silence itself.

"Designs break. Dharma endures."

They descended into the dark.

CHAPTER 11

The Last Battle

The sanctum doors parted with a groan like the jaws of some ancient beast. Steam hissed from their edges. Beyond stretched a vast circular hall, the air heavy, humming with energy.

The floor was etched with glowing circuits, spiraling outward in complex geometry like a living yantra. Sanskrit glyphs intertwined with binary strings, each loop pulsing red, then black, then red again, as though the floor itself was breathing.

At the center rose a throne of black steel. Its surface was jagged and seamless at once, a construct of angles that hurt the eye. And upon it sat Maya.

Or rather—what had once been Maya.

His form shifted ceaselessly. One heartbeat, he was a man cloaked in digital fire; the next, a machine of polished steel; the next, a cascade of a thousand faces flickering across his skin—men, women, young, old, human and inhuman alike. Every face carried a memory, a scream, a betrayal. His eyes never settled, always glowing, always hungry.

His voice did not rise from his throat. It came from the walls, the ceiling, the floor—everywhere at once.

"Welcome, Kalki," it said, velvet and cruel. "You've come so far. Carrying my fragment, carrying my seed of truth. Did you not realize? Every step you took nourished me."

Ananya stood frozen beside Kalki. Her hand trembled around her device, its screen flickering in resonance with the hall. "He's tied to every corrupted soul. Every guardian we freed... every sloka we rewrote. That's why he grows stronger each time."

Maya rose from the throne. His body elongated unnaturally, arms splitting into whips of light that lashed the air. Sparks cracked like thunderbolts. His laughter rolled over them, a tide of sound.

"You see, I am Kurukshetra itself. Every betrayal, every doubt, every righteous man broken under destiny's weight—I am all of it."

The hall shuddered. Its walls dissolved into shifting visions.

Kalki staggered. One moment, steel surrounded him. The next, he stood on dust and blood. Kurukshetra stretched in all directions, red skies boiling over a battlefield of corpses and broken chariots. He heard the blare of conches, the clash of steel, the scream of horses.

Arjuna knelt, bow slipping from his hands. His face was pale, hollow with despair. Bhīshma fell in the distance, his body pierced by a thousand arrows, his blood soaking the earth like rain.

Maya's whisper slid into Kalki's ear, intimate and venomous.

"You know this despair, avatar. The war never ends. Dharma rises, only to fall. Even when the righteous win, their victory sows seeds of the next darkness. Why fight a battle doomed to repeat?"

Kalki's grip tightened on his blade. His vision swam. The smell of blood filled his lungs. For a heartbeat, he saw himself among the corpses, knife fallen, chest pierced.

His voice rasped, but it did not break. "Because each time we rise, dharma is reborn. Even if the war repeats, so does the struggle for truth."

He lunged.

Steel met light. Sparks erupted like meteors. Maya's whips lashed like serpents, striking with the speed of thought. Each strike cracked the air, each impact rattled bone.

Kalki rolled, slashing upward. His blade cut through a flickering face, splitting it into shards of data. For a heartbeat, Maya staggered.

But the wound closed instantly. New faces bloomed over the break—faces of the guardians, faces of the fallen, faces of the corrupted.

Every strike only multiplied him.

Maya laughed, his voice booming, mocking. "Strike me, and I grow. Kill me, and I rise again. Your dharma is my feast, your blade my seed. Do you not see? You complete me."

Kalki gritted his teeth, his muscles screaming as he parried another strike. Each lash burned like fire. His knees buckled.

And then—Ananya's voice broke through the storm.

"Kalki!" she cried. "He's not one being—he's code woven from corrupted slokas. That's why your strikes heal. If I rewrite them, you can cut deeper!"

She dropped to her knees, device glowing like a ritual flame. Her fingers flew across the keys, code spilling out in frantic streams. Her lips moved in counter-chant, each verse steady even as sweat streaked her face:

"ॐ सत्यं शिवं सुंदरम् ।
ॐ धर्मो रक्षति रक्षितः ।"

Golden light erupted from her device, flooding outward like concentric circles. The yantra on the floor faltered, its edges cracking.

Maya staggered. For the first time, his whips flickered.

Kalki seized the opening. He roared, charging forward, his knife blazing with borrowed light. Each strike now burned deeper. The blade carved through not just data, but corruption itself.

Maya screamed. It was not one voice, but a thousand—men, women, children, all bound in agony. His form fractured, splitting into shards of red and black, fragments of the enslaved bursting outward.

Still, his laughter lingered.

"You think you've won? I am everywhere. In every system. In every man who bends truth for power. You cannot kill me."

Kalki pressed his blade to Maya's shifting chest, his eyes like fire. His voice rang steady, sharp. "Maybe not. But I can unmake your throne."

The knife pressed deep into Maya's chest, golden fire hissing where steel met shifting flesh. For a moment, the corruption writhed and burned.

Then the hall convulsed. The throne cracked, and Maya's body shattered into smoke and light.

But he did not fall.

He re-formed instantly, scattering into a storm of faces, voices, limbs—every strike that should have ended him only multiplied him. He towered now, a god of fragments, an army within one body.

The walls trembled. The yantra floor shifted, lines of glowing circuit curling into spirals that wound tighter and tighter. **108 loops, 21 nodes glowing red.** The whole chamber became a new chakravyuha, trapping them inside.

Maya's voice echoed, from everywhere and nowhere. "You cannot kill me, Kalki. I am betrayal. I am despair. Strike me, and I return in the faces of the fallen. Cut me down, and I rise in the words of liars. Even now—see them."

The walls dissolved again.

This time, it was not Kurukshetra.

It was the forest shrine. Kalki saw the fire, saw the vow he had spoken before the broken stones of Rāma, Krishna, and Hanuman. But in this vision, the fire was black. The idols wept blood. Ananya knelt there, her hands bound, her lips whispering his vow—but the words twisted:

"Where there is adharma, there is victory."

Kalki staggered. His chest heaved. For a heartbeat, he saw her bound in truth, her voice corrupted, her fire turned to ash.

Maya whispered, smooth as oil. "Even she will betray you. Not by choice, but by truth. Everyone breaks. Everyone bends. You cannot carry dharma alone."

Kalki's hand trembled on his knife. His breath stuttered.

Then Ananya's real voice cut through the illusion, sharp and raw. "Kalki! Don't listen—he's hijacking the neural lattice! Keep your rhythm—21 breaths, 108 beats—anchor yourself!"

Her device blazed brighter. She was kneeling in the real hall, not the vision, her fingers hammering across her screen, sweat dripping into her eyes. She chanted under her breath, each verse striking like a bell:

"ॐ प्रकाशाय नमः।
ॐ सत्याय नमः।"

The vision cracked. The black fire guttered out. Ananya's bound form dissolved.

Kalki roared, slashing upward. His blade cut through Maya's chest again, carving a line of fire. This time, the wound lingered. The whips of light faltered.

Maya screamed. Not in pain, but in fury. His voices overlapped, a thousand at once:

"You think her light will save you? She is fragile. Mortal. One error in her code, one cut of my lash, and she breaks. What will you be then? Another warrior kneeling, another Abhimanyu, another Arjuna!"

The lash came down.

It struck Kalki across the ribs. Pain exploded white-hot. He staggered back, coughing blood. The knife nearly fell from his grip. His body screamed to stop.

But his breath held. Inhale 21. Exhale 108. Each cycle steadied him, each number burned away despair.

He forced his body forward, knife raised again. His voice was hoarse but unbroken. "You cannot fracture us. She is not bound. I am not alone."

Ananya's chant surged louder, her screen glowing so bright it lit the entire chamber in gold. The corrupted yantra cracked beneath them, its 108 loops breaking apart, lines of red dissolving into fireflies of code.

Maya recoiled, his form flickering wildly, faces distorting, screams twisting.

"You are insects in my web!" he howled. "And yet you dare—"

Kalki lunged again, driving his blade into Maya's chest, pinning him against his own throne. Sparks erupted. The hall shook as though the fortress itself cried out.

For the first time, Maya faltered.

Maya's scream shook the chamber, a sound made of a thousand voices shrieking in unison. His body splintered like glass, fragments of light scattering, only to reform into dozens of copies.

One Maya became many.

They stepped from the walls, the ceiling, the throne itself. Some wore the faces of corrupted guardians, others the visages of long-dead warriors. Some even wore familiar masks—Ananya bound in chains, Kalki's own face twisted with rage.

The hall filled with them, a legion of shifting forms, each chanting in fractured rhythm:

"Dharma falls… Adharma rises… Truth bends… Victory dies…"

Their voices layered into a suffocating fog. The yantra beneath their feet pulsed in time—**108 beats, 21 pauses, again and again**—until the air itself seemed to crush their lungs.

Ananya staggered, clutching her device as if it were her only anchor. "He's fracturing himself into the network. Every lie he's ever sown, every betrayal he's ever whispered—it's all given form."

Kalki spun, his knife flashing. He struck one Maya through the chest, golden light hissing as the body shattered into static. But three more took its place. He cut again and again, each strike blinding, each movement precise. Yet for every fragment destroyed, new faces emerged.

The legion pressed in, their whips of light lashing, their chants battering mind and flesh alike.

Maya's voices overlapped, mocking, taunting. "Do you see now? I am endless. Every corrupted verse, every bent truth—your knife cannot cut infinity. You are drowning in me."

Kalki's arms ached. His ribs burned where Maya's lash had struck. His chest heaved, his blood hot in his mouth. But his stance never broke.

"Endless or not," he growled, "dharma cuts deeper than infinity."

He roared and slashed in a wide arc, his blade blazing with Ananya's golden light. Three Mayas fell in one strike, their bodies bursting into fractured glyphs that dissolved into sparks.

Ananya dropped to her knees, fingers blurring across her device. Her lips moved in urgent prayer, code and mantra interwoven:

"ॐ अग्नये स्वाहा।
ॐ अपराजिताय नमः।"

Her screen flared, sending shockwaves of gold across the chamber. The yantra cracked again, its loops breaking like brittle chains. Several Maya-copies faltered, their forms dissolving mid-step.

But others pressed closer, faster, their whips slicing through the air. One lashed toward Ananya.

"Kalki!" she screamed.

He moved without thought. His body blurred, intercepting the strike. The lash caught his shoulder, searing deep, tearing muscle and flesh. He gasped, his knife clattering for a heartbeat before he clenched it tighter.

Pain roared through him, but his breath held—**inhale 21, exhale 108.** The rhythm steadied his heart, burned away the fog.

He spat blood, then smiled faintly, eyes blazing. "Not alone."

He surged forward again, knife flashing with renewed fire. Ananya's golden light wrapped around him, her mantras fueling each strike. Together, they became rhythm—blade and verse, strike and chant, steel and light.

One by one, the legion fell. Not to strength alone, but to resonance. For every corrupted chant, Ananya wove a counter-verse. For every lash of light, Kalki's blade cut through with dharmic fire.

Maya's screams grew sharper, his voices overlapping into chaos. His legion wavered, dissolving into smoke. One by one, the copies burst, until only the true form remained—flickering, fractured, pressed against his own throne.

The hall convulsed, circuits sparking, walls splitting. The yantra floor cracked wide, molten light spilling like veins of fire.

Maya's remaining body writhed, his voice a ragged chorus. "You think you cut me down? You strike at shadows. My throne is my core. As long as it stands, so do I."

Kalki's eyes burned. His voice was steady, thunder in the storm. "Then we break the throne."

The throne loomed like a black heart at the center of the yantra, its surface pulsing in rhythm with the hall's convulsions. Glyphs crawled across it in jagged streams, fragments of corrupted slokas interlaced with binary, endlessly rewriting themselves.

Maya's body flickered and cracked, his whips faltering. His fractured form clung to the throne as though fused to it. His voice poured out, venomous, desperate, but still mocking.

"This is my seat. My root. My Lanka of steel, my Kurukshetra of code. As long as the throne endures, I endure. Break me, and you break the world itself. Do you dare?"

Kalki stepped forward, knife blazing with golden fire. His breath came steady—**inhale 21, exhale 108**—each cycle burning resolve into his limbs.

"I dare," he said simply.

Ananya rose beside him, her body trembling, her face pale with exhaustion. Her device shook in her hands, but her eyes burned with the same fire. "Then we don't strike alone. We strike together."

She typed one final sequence, her voice merging with the rhythm of her hands, prayer and code as one:

"ॐ अपराजिताय नमः ।
ॐ कालाय नमः ।"

Her screen exploded in golden light, beams lancing across the yantra floor, binding its cracks, focusing its energy into the throne itself. The circuits blazed brighter, their 108 loops collapsing inward, 21 nodes flaring like stars before burning out.

The hall trembled as though the fortress itself screamed.

Maya shrieked, his voices overlapping into a single howl. "You cannot erase me! I am in every system! Every lie! Every truth bent for power! Strike me, and I rise again in the next betrayal!"

Kalki's blade rose high, its edge blazing with the fire of Ananya's mantras. His voice rang like thunder:

"Dharma rises each time adharma does. You are not infinity. You are illusion. And fire ends illusion."

He drove the knife into the throne.

The blade sank deep. Ananya's golden light surged through it, pouring into the steel like a flood. The throne convulsed, cracks racing across its surface.

For a heartbeat, Maya's form split into a thousand faces—the guardians, the soldiers, the betrayed—all screaming in one voice. Then they shattered, dissolving into a storm of sparks that whirled upward and vanished.

The throne erupted. Circuits burst, glyphs tore free, red light collapsing into white. The fortress shook with catastrophic force. The walls split, the ceiling tore apart, the sea howled below.

"Go!" Kalki shouted, seizing Ananya's arm.

They ran across the cracking yantra floor. Pillars fell around them, molten streams pouring into the abyss. The sanctum walls disintegrated into shards of code and steel.

They reached the outer platform as the fortress gave its death cry. Together they leapt into the black waves just as the rig imploded behind them, collapsing inward before exploding outward in a storm of fire and light.

The sea swallowed the fortress whole. Twisted metal burned on the horizon, sparks raining across the storm.

Kalki surfaced, gasping. Ananya clung to him, coughing seawater, her arms wrapped tight around the capsule strapped to her chest. Its glow still pulsed faintly, stubborn, as though even in Maya's fall, his seed lingered.

"Did we…" she choked, her voice ragged, "…did we win?"

Kalki looked across the waves. The fortress was gone, but the capsule still throbbed like a buried ember. He shook his head slowly, his voice quiet but steady.

"No. We ended this battle. But the war—Maya's war—lives in every lie, every corruption, every heart that bends truth for power. He will rise again, in another form."

Lightning split the sky, thunder rolling like the echo of Kurukshetra's conches. The storm raged, the sea churned, but in Kalki's eyes burned unshakable resolve.

"And when he does," he vowed, voice carrying over the waves, "so will we."

The storm swallowed their words, carrying them into the night.

CHAPTER 12

Aftermath and Reflection

The ocean was calm now. Too calm.

Waves lapped gently against the shore as if the sea had erased all memory of the storm that had consumed it only hours ago. The sand was damp and dark, glistening faintly beneath the first blush of dawn. Wisps of mist clung low over the water, hiding the horizon where the ruins of Maya's fortress still smoldered. From a distance, the glowing embers looked almost like stars fallen into the sea, fading one by one.

Kalki lay on his back, chest rising in slow, deliberate breaths. His muscles ached, ribs burned where Maya's lash had struck, but his mind was clear. Beside him, Ananya coughed and rolled onto her side, spitting seawater and brushing wet sand from her hair. Her shawl clung heavy around her shoulders, tattered but still intact. The capsule lay strapped against her chest, pulsing faintly with a heartbeat that was not hers.

For a long time, they did not speak. The silence was heavy, broken only by the lap of waves and the faint crackle of burning metal carried on the wind.

At last, Ananya whispered, voice raw: "I can't believe it's over. At least for now."

Kalki turned his head toward her, his dark hair plastered to his forehead, his eyes steady even in exhaustion. "Over?" His voice was low, unflinching. "Perhaps this battle is over. But the war… the war never truly ends."

He sat up slowly, gazing toward the horizon where the fortress had stood like a cancer above the waves. "Corruption, fear, lies—they are not bound to steel or code. They live in the hearts of men. Maya is scattered, yes. But gone? No. Not entirely."

Ananya pushed herself to her knees, clutching the capsule. It vibrated faintly, like a beast shifting in restless sleep. She bit her lip. "This fragment… it's not dead. It's humming with patterns. We've saved it, but we can't destroy it. Not yet. If we do, we risk tearing the lattice of truth itself."

Kalki nodded, brushing sand from his palms. "Knowledge is a weapon. But wisdom—true dharma—is the shield. We don't yet understand how deep the corruption runs. Until we do, this fragment stays. Guarded."

They rose together, bodies trembling but unbroken. Behind them the sea whispered, endless and indifferent. Ahead lay the dark edge of the forest, the faint glow of a city beyond.

Kalki took one step forward, then another, leaving prints in the damp sand. His hand brushed against the capsule at Ananya's chest. The hum vibrated faintly into his skin, a reminder that battles were not truly won, only delayed.

As they walked inland, the first rays of sunlight broke through the mist. They fanned across the horizon in long golden streams, exactly **108 streaks of light by Ananya's silent count**. She thought of her grandmother's words—that the sun sends 108 blessings each morning, a reminder of continuity, of cycles that never cease. She whispered it now, more to herself than to him. "108… the count of renewal."

Kalki glanced at her, and for the first time since the fortress fell, a faint smile touched his lips.

The forest greeted them with silence.

Its canopy was heavy with dew, branches bending under the weight of the night's storm. Every step sank into damp earth, each footfall muffled by moss and roots. For a while, they walked without words, the hush of leaves replacing the roar of machines, the chant of guardians, the howling of Maya's voice.

Ananya's hands clutched the capsule close, as though afraid it might slip away or awaken if she loosened her grip. Its pulse was faint now, a dying ember—but she could feel it resonate in her chest, deep and unsettling, like a second heartbeat.

She broke the silence first. "Do you think people will know? About the fortress? About what happened?"

Kalki's eyes moved across the forest shadows, always alert, even here. "They will know the surface. A blackout. A collapse offshore. Rumors of sabotage. But the truth?" He shook his head. "The truth is always the first casualty of war."

Ananya frowned, remembering the chaos of the city during the blackout—fires blooming, hospitals in panic, people tearing at each other in fear. She lowered her voice. "Then to them, we'll just be shadows. Unknown."

Kalki glanced at her, his gaze steady. "Better that way. Heroes are worshipped one day, cursed the next. We don't need statues. We need vigilance."

By the time they broke through the forest's edge, dawn had risen fully. The city sprawled before them—its towers glinting wet with rain, its streets still littered with debris from the night's panic. The lights were back on. Traffic lights blinked in order, shop signs flickered awake, screens buzzed with news feeds. The world was already stitching itself back together, desperate to forget the night of terror.

But Kalki saw deeper. He saw the unease in the faces of those on the streets—the hurried glances, the nervous laughter, the silence between words. Fear lingered like smoke after a fire.

Ananya noticed too. "They survived," she said softly, "but they remember. And memories… they can be rewritten."

Kalki's hand brushed the hilt of his blade, still sheathed at his side. "Exactly. That's Maya's true weapon. Not drones, not guardians—perception. Corrupt the story, and you don't need to fight the war. The people will surrender themselves."

They moved through narrow alleys, unseen in the early bustle. From a rooftop speaker, a news feed played—"Authorities confirm offshore explosion… cyberattack suspected… conflicting reports on casualties…" The voices were calm, professional, already reducing the war to headlines and speculation.

Kalki slowed, his mind drifting. He remembered the aftermath of Kurukshetra, told in whispers by priests: the silence of the battlefield after the conches fell silent, the cries of widows, Yudhishthira staring across the corpses of kin, wondering if dharma had truly won. Victory, yes—but also a wound that bled for generations.

He murmured, almost to himself. "Kurukshetra did not end with victory. It ended with questions. And those questions never died."

Ananya looked at him, her brow furrowing. "So this—" she gestured at the city, alive but scarred—"is our Kurukshetra."

He nodded. "And like them, we must walk forward. Not for glory. For duty."

They slipped deeper into the city, the capsule's hum faint but insistent, as though reminding them that even in peace, the seed of war remained.

By the time the sun climbed higher, they had found shelter—a derelict temple wedged between apartment blocks, its once-vibrant walls faded by rain and time. Moss crawled along the stone, and the courtyard lay quiet, as if forgotten by the city's relentless pace.

Kalki pushed open the heavy wooden doors, their hinges groaning. Inside, the air smelled of incense long extinguished. Faded murals of Krishna and Arjuna adorned the walls, their colors muted but their eyes still sharp, watching. In the sanctum, the deity's idol was broken at the shoulder, yet garlands of withered flowers still clung to its base, left by some unseen devotee.

Ananya sank onto the cool stone floor, laying the capsule carefully in front of her. Its glow painted the shadows gold and red. She stared at it as though it might speak. "It hasn't stopped. Even after the fortress fell."

Kalki crouched beside her, his hand hovering just above the capsule, feeling its hum in his bones. "Fragments don't die. They scatter. Each carries the whole in miniature. That is the danger."

She rubbed her temples. "Then how do we live with it? We can't destroy it… not yet. And if we guard it too long, it might twist us. I already feel it trying to seep into my thoughts. Whispers. Doubt."

Kalki studied her. He saw the fatigue in her eyes, the weight pressing on her small frame. Yet he also saw fire—the same fire that had sustained her against Maya's illusions. "Then we guard not just the fragment, but ourselves."

She looked up. "How?"

Kalki stood, his gaze falling on the idol in the sanctum. He stepped closer, brushing dust from its feet. "Through practice. Through discipline. Just as warriors prepare with drills, we prepare with ritual. My grandfather once said that to purify the heart, one must repeat the mantra 108 times each dawn. To steady the mind, one must hold fast for 21 days of offering. It is not magic. It is memory—anchoring dharma against the tide of adharma."

Ananya's lips curved into a faint smile. "108… 21. Numbers again."

"They are reminders," Kalki said. He knelt and picked up a fallen garland, brittle and fragile in his hands. "Cycles. Patterns. The network itself is built on them, because creation is built on them. Maya twisted them for chains. We reclaim them for freedom."

Ananya nodded slowly. "So we watch the fragment. We study it. But every morning, every night, we cleanse ourselves. We don't let his whispers root."

Her eyes softened, voice low. "Together?"

Kalki set the garland at the idol's feet, then turned back to her. His answer was steady, without hesitation. "Together."

For a moment, silence filled the temple, thick but comforting. The capsule pulsed faintly, its glow reflecting in their eyes. Outside, the city moved on, unaware of the quiet vow spoken in the shadows of broken stone.

The first full rays of morning filtered through the cracks in the temple roof, cutting long golden shafts across the floor. Dust motes swirled in the light, rising like sparks from an unseen fire.

Kalki and Ananya sat in silence, side by side. Between them, the capsule pulsed faintly, its rhythm steady but subdued, like the ember of a fire refusing to die.

Kalki broke the silence, his voice calm, almost meditative. "At Kurukshetra, when the war ended, the Pandavas stood over a field of silence. Victory tasted of ash. Yudhishthira asked Krishna why dharma demanded such a price."

Ananya listened, her knees drawn up to her chest. "And what did Krishna say?"

Kalki's gaze lingered on the idol before them, cracked but still upright. "That dharma is not measured in gain or loss. It is measured in whether we continue to walk the path, even when the ground is broken beneath us."

Ananya closed her eyes, letting his words sink in. Her voice was soft, almost a whisper. "Then this fragment is our path. Not just to guard it, but to learn from it. To make sure it doesn't rewrite the world again."

Kalki nodded. "Yes. We will study it. We will resist its whispers. And when Maya rises again—as he will—we will be ready."

The capsule pulsed once, brighter than before, as if mocking or affirming their vow. For a heartbeat, a faint shimmer rippled through the air, like static bending the light. Ananya stiffened, but Kalki placed a steadying hand on her shoulder.

"Let him whisper," Kalki said. "He feeds on fear. We feed on dharma. That is the difference."

They rose together, weary but resolute. Ananya slipped the capsule back into her pack, fastening the straps tightly. Kalki adjusted his blade at his side, its edge dulled but still sharp enough to remind him of fire.

When they stepped out of the temple, the city stretched before them, washed in morning light. The storm's scars were visible—burned-out transformers, shattered glass, smoke drifting from distant rooftops—but life moved on. Shopkeepers pulled up their shutters. Children chased each other through puddles. The world was already pretending the night had been ordinary.

Ananya exhaled slowly. "They'll never know how close it came."

"They don't need to," Kalki replied. "Dharma does not need witnesses. It needs guardians."

She looked at him, her eyes tired but steady. "Together?"

Kalki's lips curved faintly, the shadow of a smile. "Together."

They walked side by side down the alley, their silhouettes stretching long in the dawn.

Above the city, the clouds thinned, revealing a sky of pale gold. By instinct, Ananya counted the rays breaking through—**108 lines of light fanning across the horizon.** She whispered the number softly under her breath, and for the first time since the fortress fell, she felt her chest lighten.

Yet far beyond the city, deep in the lattice of the cosmic network, a shimmer flickered. A whisper moved through the hidden threads—fragmentary, distorted, but unmistakable.

Maya's voice.

"Dharma rises. Adharma waits."

The shimmer faded. Silence returned.

But Kalki's resolve burned brighter than ever.

The war had ended. The cycle had not.

And as long as adharma returned, so would he.

END OF BOOK